# His Ideal Match

Arlene James

Recycling programs for this product may not exist in your area.

ISBN-13: 978-0-373-81740-5

HIS IDEAL MATCH



This edition published by arrangement with Love Inspired Books.



www.Harlequin.com

**Printed in U.S.A.**

Two are better than one, because they have a good return for their labor: If either of them falls down, one can help the other up. But pity anyone who falls and has no one to help them up.

—*Ecclesiastes* 4:9–10

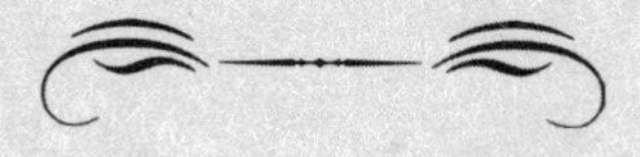

For Joseph, who has given this mom plenty of gray hair but much, much delight.

Pride is a sin to which my sons continually tempt me.

# *Chapter One*

The wrought iron gate stood ajar, so Phillip Chatam slipped into the leafy courtyard of the Downtown Bible Church of Buffalo Creek, Texas. Here, landscape lighting held back the gathering gloom of this first Thursday evening of June. Behind him rose the sanctuary in all its stylized Spanish glory. Ahead of him, a walkway wound through the trees and flower beds. It was a peaceful place, but had he not promised his aunts—the renowned seventy-five-year-old triplets of Chatam House—that he would attend tonight's grief support meeting, he would not be here.

When his aunts had politely but firmly insisted that he attend this meeting, he could have told them that they were mistaken in their assumption that grief and fear had driven him away from his occupation of the past several years and into this state of ennui, where he had languished for the past five weeks. Of course, he grieved the deaths of his friends and coworkers in a fall from the mountain in Washington State where he had worked for some time. He had functioned in a daze for at least six weeks after the accident.

The company he'd worked for had brought in professional counselors, and Phillip, like the other guides and outfitters, had attended his obligatory three sessions. Like the others, he had experienced moments of fear and discomfort on his next climb, and truth be told, he had secretly welcomed such emotions. Guiding tourists on mountain climbs had become old hat. Fear had at least added an element of excitement to the process. The apprehension had rapidly dissipated, however, and he had known then that it was time to move on. But to what?

For eight months he had gone through the motions. The whole time, he'd been looking for the next challenge, the next adventure. In the past, something had always cropped up. This time, though, he hadn't been able to wait on it. This time, he'd started to worry that his lack of enthusiasm for the work was going to get someone else hurt. He'd walked away in the middle of the season, just packed up his stuff and left Seattle for Texas. He'd spent the past five weeks at Chatam House, the antebellum mansion where his aunties had lived their entire lives and the lodestone of the large, far-flung Chatam family.

During that time, his parents had harassed him almost daily about finding a "real" job, and his aunts had worried that he was ignoring his grief. The least he could do, given that the aunties had opened their home to him, was assuage their concern by schlepping downtown to a meeting of the DBC Grief Support Group.

He followed the signs along a hallway and down a flight of stairs to the meeting room in the basement. Soft instrumental music and muted light greeted him as he passed through the open doorway. A pair of older women smiled at him from the counter laden with cookies, coffee and water. His gaze swept the softly lit room, taking in the other occupants. Most were older than him. A boy and girl in their late teens or early twenties appeared to be siblings. Hub, Phillip's elderly uncle and a retired minister, swooped in with arms spread wide in welcome.

"Phillip! So good to see you." Reaching up to slide an arm across Phillip's shoulders, Hub turned to address the milling group. "My nephew Phillip Chatam is joining us tonight. He's come home to Texas from Seattle."

Most people nodded and offered taut smiles, but the two women at the refreshment table beamed as they carried over napkin-wrapped cookies and a disposable cup of coffee strong enough to anchor a grappling hook. Phillip accepted both with self-conscious nods before dropping down onto the nearest folding chair. About a dozen of them had been arranged in a horseshoe shape. The other attendees quietly took up seats, leaving several empty, including the one on the end to Phillip's left.

"Let us begin with silent prayer," said Hub.

Everyone hushed. Several moments ticked by while Phillip tried to think of a prayer, finally coming up with, *God, be with the families of those who died.*

It was the same prayer he'd prayed on the day of the accident. He didn't figure it would do much good. It seemed to Phillip that God was too busy to pay attention to him, but it couldn't hurt to send up a prayer now and again.

Someone slipped into the empty chair on Phillip's left, derailing his train of thought and sharpening his senses. Before he could stop himself, he turned his head, just enough so that he could see a portion of a feminine form from the corner of his eye.

A pair of worn but clean white canvas sneakers came into view, followed by the frayed hems of slender faded jeans. A pair of delicate, feminine hands rested in casual but prayerful repose atop one jeaned knee, but that was as much as Phillip could see.

Several long minutes later, Hub said, "Amen."

"We have another newcomer," Hub announced, engaging the latest arrival with a welcoming nod. He reached out a gnarled hand for a gentle shake. "I'm Pastor Hub." He went around the room, naming everyone in order. "This is Phillip, Mr. Edgar, the Lallys, Margaret, Sandra, Miss Clara and Bernice."

Turning to the woman at his side, Phillip smiled and tried not to stare. She was beautiful, in a wide-eyed, elegant way that belied the casual twist of her golden-brown hair and slightly shabby clothing. Without a speck of cosmetics, she took his breath away.

Phillip suddenly wished he had shaved. His brown hair was so dark it was almost black, and the hair on his face gave him a constant five-o'clock shadow, always appearing between shaves. In fact, within three weeks' time, he could have a beard heavy enough to obliterate the cleft chin that marked every adult Chatam and the dimples that his mother so adored.

He unconsciously fingered the deep cleft in his chin now as he took in the generous smattering of freckles across his new neighbor's tiny nose and high cheekbones. Wide, naturally rosy lips revealed neat, white teeth without quite smiling, and tawny hair wisped about an oval face with a delicately pointed chin. She had unusual eyes of a deep velvet blue, thickly fringed in dark gold lashes. She looked young, early to mid-twenties, but wore a maturity that made her seem older. He couldn't take his eyes off her.

She introduced herself to the group in a husky, whispery voice. "I'm Carissa Hopper."

Phillip shifted in his chair. Feeling like a teen boy with an unexpected crush, he concentrated on his hands. Rough and hard, they were no longer the slender-fingered hands that his mother had once declared those of a pianist or surgeon. He concentrated on a tiny jagged scar on the side of one knuckle where a crampon had sliced his glove as the climber above him had struggled to find his footing.

Shaking himself, he sat up straighter and listened as Hub instructed everyone to tell why they were there. When Phillip's turn came, he cleared his throat and muttered, "Two of my friends and a client were in a rock-climbing accident over eight months ago. They fell when a cliff face suddenly gave way."

The woman beside him displayed no such hesitancy to speak, declaring forthrightly, "My husband was killed almost four years ago when a truck he was working beneath fell on him. I'm here now, frankly, just to please certain family members." She went on to explain, "Times are tough right now. They're worried about me."

Phillip spoke out of the corner of his mouth. "Same deal with me. Here to please family."

If Carissa Hopper thought that this gave them more in common than the others present, she gave no sign of it.

Hub began to speak about how tough times could affect grief by exaggerating or covering over it. Those who were regulars to the group offered up personal stories illustrating the point in one way or another. Phillip barely heard them. He was too busy planning how to get to know Carissa Hopper better.

Hub closed the meeting with a few well-chosen words on overcoming grief. "Don't wait for others to minister to you. Do something for someone else," he said.

That made sense to Phillip, but it didn't apply to him. He wasn't sad, just uncertain what to do next. Surely he'd come up with something before his money ran out. A decent accountant, he knew how to make his bucks last, which was why he was currently enjoying the haven of Chatam House. And attending grief support meetings to appease his aunties.

As the session broke up, he rose to follow the lovely Carissa from the room, rehearsing conversational icebreakers in his head.

Before he could catch up to her, however, his uncle laid claim to him. "Phillip, can you help with these chairs?"

Glancing at the folding chairs being loaded onto a long, rolling rack, Phillip frowned inwardly. "In a minute, Uncle Hub. Be right back."

He dashed from the room, only to find the hall empty. Racing up the stairs, he tore through the building, sure he would catch her before she reached the courtyard, but she must have gone another way, for when he pushed through the door, he found himself alone on the softly lit path.

Disappointed, he heaved a sigh. Well, maybe next week.

*Lord,* he thought, *if You're listening, if it matters, I'd like to see that woman again. Please.*

In fact, he'd attend more grief support meetings on the chance that he'd see her again.

"But I don't *want* to stay here," nine-year-old Nathan grumbled, glaring at his mother through his wire-rimmed glasses. They were too small for his face, reminding Carissa that he needed to have his eyes reexamined. All the more reason for this visit. She just had to have some uninterrupted work time. Otherwise, she was going to lose her job.

Selling technical service over the phone from

home wasn't the perfect job. For one thing, it didn't pay particularly well. For another, when home was a two-bedroom apartment shared by two adults and three children, chaos was the norm, and that made it difficult for her to meet her monthly quota. On the other hand, working from home meant that she didn't have to pay for child care. Still, no quota, no job—which was why she had finally accepted her aunt's offer to babysit. She just hoped that her mother didn't get wind of it. The last thing she needed was for Alexandra to show up, offering her limited, strings-attached services.

Carissa looked at the stately building. Chatam House, where her uncle Chester and aunt Hilda lived and worked, was a mansion. Old and elegant, it was fronted by a deep, cool porch supported by majestic white columns, with redbrick walkways and steps. Well, she had no time to moon over tall windows, many rooms and dark, loamy beds bursting with flowers.

"I have to work today, Nathan, and Grandpa's doctor says he needs some peace and quiet so he can rest. You'll have fun with Uncle Chester and Aunt Hilda today."

Holding each of the younger children, Tucker and Grace, by the hand, Carissa led the way around the house. She'd been told to park in front to keep from blocking the carport, or porte cochere, as Chester called it. They stepped off the walkway and into gravel, trudging along beside the mansion and past a bronze Subaru Outback to the side door. While she knocked on the bright yellow door with the old-fashioned fan-shaped window above it, the kids crowded onto the porch behind her, bumping against big terra-cotta pots spilling over with flowers.

"Hang on!" called a muffled voice after a moment. "I'm coming."

Carissa backed up as far as she could and folded her arms to hide the empty hole in her simple white blouse where the button was missing. The door opened, and a tall man stepped up to the threshold. Make that a *very* tall man.

A smile in place, she spoke as she tilted her head back. "Hello. I'm—"

"Carissa Hopper," he supplied, grinning.

At the same time, she exclaimed, "Phillip?"

They both followed with "What are you doing here?"

He chuckled. "I live here." While she blinked at that, he thrust his hand forward. "It's Phillip *Chatam,* by the way."

She shook hands with him, remembering only at the last instant to leave one arm folded across her middle. "I—I didn't realize."

He held her hand in his big, hard one. "You came in late to the meeting last night. I guess

Hub didn't say my last name when he introduced us." Pulling free, she grasped her elbows, hiding the empty hole in her blouse and separating herself from Phillip's warmth. "What can I do for you?" he asked, rocking back on his heels.

"My aunt offered to watch my kids today."

"Your aunt?"

"Hilda Worth. Chester Worth is my father's brother."

Phillip Chatam's eyebrows jumped halfway up his forehead. "Chester and Hilda are your family? So, *they're* the ones who sent you to the—"

"Yes," she interrupted. She didn't want the kids to know where she'd been. *Grief* was a word they'd heard too often in their young lives.

"I see. Knowing them, I'm sure they've cleared this with my aunts."

"Yes, um, assuming your aunts are the Chatam sisters."

"Yup. And Pastor Hub is my uncle."

"Well, that explains a lot."

He flashed a stunning smile. "I'm sure it does." Dropping his gaze, he asked, "And who do we have here?"

Stepping back, she pushed the children forward. "This is Nathan," she said, dragging him in front of her. "He's nine." He shrugged and wiggled out of her grasp. She then placed both hands atop his brother's slender shoulders. "Tucker.

He's seven. And last but not least…" Reaching down with one hand, she cupped her daughter's cheek as the girl's head pressed against her leg. "This is Grace, who's four."

Phillip gave the children a smile and lifted his gaze to Carissa once more. *Typical,* she thought sourly. No man had any interest in another man's children, as she had learned the hard way.

"Well, come in. Hilda's in the kitchen."

Cautiously, Carissa followed him, sweeping the children along in front of her so that they formed a buffer between her and this too-attractive Chatam. She'd long ago decided to keep her distance from such men. Several times since her husband Tom's death, she'd let herself be drawn to men with the same rough masculine appeal as her late husband, only to find herself unceremoniously dumped as soon as they realized that she wasn't going to settle for anything short of marriage. She'd finally learned her lesson when the last guy had informed her that a man might marry a woman with one kid or even two, but never *three.* That very day, she had resigned herself to the realities of widowhood and resolved to keep temptation at a safe distance.

If she hadn't been running late, she would never have taken the chair next to Phillip. Only as the brief introductions had been made had she realized her mistake. Those copper eyes, set deeply into a lean, bronzed face heavily shadowed with a dark beard and carved with dimples and a cleft chin, had taken her breath away. Hair the color of coffee and a nose that showed signs of having been broken at some point added the very type of ruggedness that appealed to her. Combined with his long-limbed height—at least three or four inches over six feet—and broad shoulders, he was definitely one of the best-looking men she'd ever met. She'd decided right then to forget all about grief support, no matter what her family said—only to find herself face-to-face with the man this morning.

He led them down the hallway to a swinging door, which he pushed wide, calling out, "Hilda, you have company."

A clatter of metal heralded her aunt's appearance in the doorway. Swathed in a damp apron over a voluminous dress made of some small, gray-brown print almost the exact color as her thin, straight, ear-length hair, Hilda exuded the aromas of a bakery.

She reached over the children to envelop Carissa in her hefty arms. Stooping, she did the same with the children, all three at once. "I've set up the sunroom for the kids. But first, how was the meeting last night?"

Phillip Chatam shifted beside Carissa. She felt his interest, and that made this discussion all the more difficult. Managing a tiny smile, she recalled the words that she had prepared earlier in anticipation of this moment.

"You're right, Aunt Hilda. Pastor Hub is a very wise man. I especially liked what he had to say about helping others."

"As a way of getting our minds off our own sorrows," Phillip supplied.

Hilda's narrow gaze sharpened. "You were there, too, Phillip?"

"Yes. The aunties thought I would benefit."

"Seems we were both there at the urging of family," Carissa said drily.

"I know it's going to help," Hilda exclaimed, throwing out her arms. Hooking one mighty appendage about each of their necks, she gave both a squeeze. Carissa winced as her head knocked against Phillip's.

The wretch chuckled. "Hilda, you're priceless."

The good-natured cook chortled then let them go.

Carissa looked away—and caught her eldest son's disapproving frown. She couldn't think of anything that Nathan did approve of these days, but she couldn't really blame him. Since they'd lost the house, they'd had to move into her poor father's tiny two-bedroom apartment. There was no space for a growing boy to take a deep breath, let alone play. Her father's illness didn't help, either, though he never complained about the noise or chaos. Nathan, more than the other children, understood what his grandfather's illness meant. It was no wonder he wasn't happy.

She thought of her aunt's and uncle's urgings to get the children into church again and wondered if that would help. They'd gradually fallen away after Tom's death. She had struggled to get an infant and two rambunctious little boys dressed in their Sunday best and out the door week after week on her own, but what was her excuse now that the children were nine, seven and four?

A clock chimed somewhere, bringing Carissa out of her thoughts.

"I need to get to work. Let me help you settle the children."

"This way. This way," Hilda urged, waddling off down the hall. She began detailing the preparations she'd made: coloring books and crayons, games, puzzles, toys. She even had a box of dress-up clothes gleaned from "Miss Odelia's big closet upstairs." Little Grace beamed with delight.

Carissa marched the children into the room, hugged each one and thanked Phillip Chatam for his assistance. Ready to focus on what lay before her, she began to mentally plan her workday as she started back down the long hallway. She just needed one good day without distractions to ensure her job for another month. She knew her stuff; she could sell enough tech support to see her family through the immediate crisis. One good day on the telephone without three children bouncing off the walls of a too-small apartment—that was all she asked.

Thanking God for an aunt and uncle willing to help out, she tried not to worry. Hilda could manage three small children, and it was a very large house. Surely they would be all right for one day. With a man like Phillip Chatam around, she dared not risk more, and the same went for grief support meetings.

She didn't need those meetings anyway. Tom had been gone for four years now; emotionally, she'd come to terms with his loss long ago. Aunt Hilda and Uncle Chester were trying to help her prepare for what was to come, of course, but Carissa didn't believe in borrowing trouble. After all, didn't the Bible say not to worry about tomorrow? Each day, according to Matthew, had enough trouble of its own. She could certainly vouch for that. It seemed to her that it was time for things to go right for a change, if only for one day.

Just one day…

## *Chapter Two*

Tiny Grace Hopper possessed a miniature version of her mother's face, framed by board-straight, light red hair cut raggedly just below her ears. That and her mother's rich blue eyes made for an adorable combination. Phillip couldn't help being entranced, just as he couldn't help being dismayed that Carissa Hopper was the mother of three kids.

Children had never figured into Phillip's life. He didn't have anything against them, he just didn't feel any particular need to have them. Plus he knew less than zilch about them, even though his mother was a well-respected pediatrician. Still, he knew cute when he saw it, and Grace Hopper was cute with a capital *C*. He laughed when, upon spying a small basket, Grace hopped up and down, clapped her dainty hands and squealed, "Muffins!"

Her brother, the one *without* the glasses, ran across the room and tore into the ginger muffins with all the finesse of a starving hooligan. Before Hilda could stop him, the older boy did.

"Stop it, Tucker! That's rude."

"Ginger muffins. Mmm..." Tucker argued, his mouth full of the same.

Phillip watched as Hilda quickly parceled out the muffins then shook his head as she trundled toward him.

"You," he teased, "are a woman of mystery. I know you have a son and daughter and grandchildren, but no one ever said anything about nieces."

The fiftysomething cook waved a hand. "Silly man. Chester's brother Marshall has two girls. Carissa is the oldest." Hilda sobered then, quietly confiding, "No one has a clue where the youngest, Lyla, is. Crying shame. Marshall isn't well. *Lung cancer,*" she whispered.

"Sorry to hear that," Phillip murmured.

"I'm going to tell!"

The pounding of small feet accompanied the threat. First one small head then another dashed past Phillip and out the door.

"Tucker! Nathan!" Hilda scolded. "You come back here."

Phillip stepped out of the way, but before Hilda could squeeze past him, the boys shot through the central corridor and into the back hall. Huffing, Hilda sent Phillip an aggrieved look that he read too well. Wryly, he went after the boys. They had caught Carissa Hopper before she'd even made it out of the house and were arguing loudly about a stolen muffin.

Phillip broke into a jog as Carissa ordered, "Lower your voices. Now."

"He stole my muffin!"

"You weren't going to eat it!"

Arriving on the scene, Phillip quickly intervened. "There's plenty for everyone. No need to argue."

The older boy whipped around, snarling, "It ain't none of your business."

His mother gasped. "Nathan Alexander Hopper," she rebuked firmly. "You apologize this instant."

Sullenly, the boy dropped his head, but after a moment he muttered, "Sorry."

"I expect you to look after your brother and sister, not misbehave," Carissa went on. "You know I depend on you."

"Yes, ma'am."

"And, Tucker, you mind your manners," she instructed the younger boy.

"Yes, Mama."

"Go now, both of you."

After some grumbling, the two boys reluctantly started back down the hallway toward the sunroom. Carissa gave Phillip an exasperated look, as if he were somehow to blame, and spun sharply on one heel.

"Now, wait a minute," he began, piqued.

"I'm sorry," she snapped as he fell into step beside her. "It's just that I *have* to work."

"And that," he said, as they reached the door, "makes *me* the bad guy?"

"No," she answered drily, drawing out the single syllable even as she reached for the doorknob.

"Great," Phillip said, putting up an arm to block her way. "Then maybe you'll tell me what sort of work do you do."

"Telemarketing," she answered succinctly, folding her arms but refusing to look at him.

Phillip waited. She glanced up and huffed.

"My husband was a software engineer. He taught me everything he knew. He believed that good computer skills would ensure anyone a job. Unfortunately, in a lousy economy, without the diploma to back up those skills, no one will give me the time of day, even if I can write code better than anyone, which is why I sell tech support over the telephone rather than perform it."

"So you're good with computers, then," Phillip said.

She tossed her head, fixing him with a narrow stare. "If by 'good' you mean I can tear down a computer to its most basic elements, fix any problem, put it back together again *and* write the software that operates it, then yes, I'm good with computers." She parked her hands at her hips. "Now, what about you?"

"Oh," he answered cheerfully, "I can turn on a computer, click a mouse, even type, if you're not in a hurry."

One corner of her mouth curled in a reluctant smile. "I mean, what do you do for a living?"

"Ah. Nothing, at the moment. I used to climb mountains, but I am, as they say, between jobs."

"And I am trying *not* to be," she said pointedly.

He dropped his arm, opened the door and stepped out of the way. She swept out onto the redbrick stoop and went quickly down the steps. He had closed the door behind her before it occurred to him that he hadn't seen her vehicle parked beneath the porte cochere.

Suspecting that Hilda had told her not to park there for fear of blocking his car, he hurried through the house to the front door, stepping out onto the deep front porch in time to see Carissa Hopper climb into a battered little minivan with a missing rear hubcap and rusty passenger door handle. She drove away without so much as a wave of farewell. He wandered back into the foyer and leaned against the curled banister at the foot of the marble staircase, thinking about what she'd told him. The sound of a distant crash had him breaking into a run as a plaintive cry rose from the vicinity of the sunroom. It would only be the first of many.

Over the next two hours, Nathan and Tucker would manage to knock over a table, two chairs and a potted plant the size of a grown man. After the first altercation, Phillip decided to pitch in with the kids. Otherwise, he feared that no one would get lunch. Hilda's husband, Chester, his aunts' houseman, had driven Aunt Hypatia—or Auntie H—into town. Kent, Aunt Odelia's husband, had gone down to his pharmacy to help out his young partner, while Odelia—Auntie Od to her adoring nieces and nephews—was taking a "spa day" in their suite, and Aunt Magnolia—affectionately known as Mags—was puttering around in the flower beds, as usual. If Hilda was going to get into the kitchen, Phillip had no choice but to watch over the scamps.

The boys kept him so busy that he didn't realize Grace was missing until they did.

What could he do then but take them to look for her?

Humming to herself, Odelia Chatam Monroe swanned through the lovely mauve-and-cream sitting room of the suite that she shared with Kent, her husband of almost a year, and on into the purple bedroom, where the silk bed hangings, drapes and spread provided an appropriately romantic theme. They'd waited fifty years to marry, and they meant to enjoy every moment left to them. Pausing beside the antique Queen Anne dresser, she twitched a few gladiolus blossoms in a tall crystal vase into perfect position, before continuing into the enormous fuchsia-and-yellow bathroom to remove the cold cream from her face. After tossing aside the cucumber slices that she'd placed over her eyes, she next applied a judicious layer of makeup on her face. Finally, she removed the curlers from her thick, white hair and combed it out.

True, she was no girl, but Kent thought her beautiful. How she adored him. She took a moment to thank God for blessing her with such a husband in the twilight of her long, happy life before venturing into her closet, her favorite room in the whole house.

She noticed that she'd accidentally left the light on, but the crystal chandelier gave her such pleasure that she didn't dwell on it. Of the many material gifts that Kent had given her—this gorgeous suite, the ostentatious ring on her finger, the pool in the backyard, to name a few—the closet was her favorite, for he'd had the walls painted in color-coded stripes so that her eclectic wardrobe could be stored in a somewhat orderly fashion. She did so love clothes. Giggling, she wondered what she ought to wear for lunch. Wouldn't a gladiolus theme be fun?

An answering giggle surprised her. Odelia considered the possibility of an echo, but common sense—oh, yes, she did have some, no matter what others might say—told her that could not be so. For one thing, the racks were stuffed with clothing. For another, the room simply wasn't large enough. That meant she must not be alone.

Looking around, she said brightly, "Hello?"

To her surprise, a little head wreathed in the aqua chiffon of one of her favorite skirts popped out from a row of dresses. "Hello."

For a long moment, Odelia could do nothing but stare. The little one clomped into view, wearing a pale green knit short set, as well as a pair of Odelia's pumps over her own canvas shoes and anklets. At second glance, she also wore other bits and pieces of Odelia's wardrobe, including a gold belt worn sash-style over one shoulder and a feathered boa.

"You got snappers on your ears," the little one said.

"Snappers?"

"Turdles. Snappers turdles."

Odelia touched her earlobes, feeling her earrings. They had seemed appropriate after her gardening-mad sister had complained at breakfast that a box turtle had been snacking on her rhododendrons. "You mean, snapping turtles, I think." She had forgotten about them.

"Yep. You got 'em on your ears."

"So I do, and you have on my things." Odelia recognized a scarf and a pair of old gloves that she'd given Hilda earlier. Puzzle pieces tumbled into place. "Ah. You're Hilda's great-niece."

The girl nodded. "We're playing dress-up."

Odelia smiled, recognizing a kindred spirit. "What's your name, child?"

"Grace."

"Grace is not a full name," Odelia admonished gently. "For instance, I am Odelia Mae Chatam Monroe." Frowning, she pressed a finger against the cleft in her chin. "Or should that be Mrs. Kent Monroe? Mrs. Odelia Monroe?" Hypatia would know. Odelia waved a hand. "You may call me Miss Odelia. Now then, your name? Your full name, if you please."

"Grace Amanda Hopper," the imp said, wobbling in the shoes.

"So, you like to play dress-up, do you, Grace Amanda?"

"Best of anything."

Odelia grinned and clapped her hands. "So do I!"

Just then, a frantic male voice cried out, "Grace! Grace, where are you?"

"In here," Odelia trilled.

Phillip arrived, breathless, one boy in hand and another trailing behind with a scowl on his bespectacled face.

"Thank You, God!" Phillip gasped, rolling his eyes to the ceiling. Slumping against the doorjamb, he huffed out a breath and sucked in another before fixing Grace with a baleful glare. "Young lady, you scared the life out of me."

"I'm sorry," Grace said contritely, going to take his free hand in hers.

Odelia watched all six foot four inches of her nephew melt like so much marshmallow over a campfire. Interesting.

"Just don't take off like that again," he scolded before looking to Odelia. "I'm sorry. She got away from us."

"You are so in for it," chortled the freckle-faced, gap-toothed boy being physically restrained by Phillip.

"No, she is not," Odelia decreed, smiling down at her little guest, "but perhaps next time, she will seek permission before she goes exploring."

"Yes, ma'am," coached the older boy with glasses. Reaching around Phillip, he poked the girl.

"Yes, ma'am," little Grace echoed dutifully.

"Very well," Odelia said, waving them all out. "We'll make formal introductions at luncheon."

As Phillip towed the children away, he said, "I'm not sure what Hilda has planned for lunch."

"Whatever it is," Odelia told him brightly, following their ragtag little group into the sitting room, "I'm sure it will be lovely."

After a season of weddings, they had experienced a tranquil period at Chatam House. First had come the marriage of Phillip's older brother, Asher, and Kent's granddaughter Ellie, whose newborn daughter the family had recently welcomed. Chatam House's gardener, Garrett Willows, and his Jessa had married almost immediately afterward, with Odelia and Kent's wedding following just one month later. Shortly after that, Phillip's oldest sister, Petra, had married Garrett's friend Dale Bowen.

Two other nephews, Reeves and Chandler, and a niece, Kaylie, had met their spouses here at Chatam House. It had been months since the house had hosted company, however. Then Phillip had arrived, for no apparent reason, and here he remained, much to the disgust of his parents and the concern of his aunts. The boy just did not seem to want to work. Oh, he wasn't lazy; he just had no direction. He seemed to be waiting for some sort of inspiration to strike—or for some grand adventure to present itself.

Hypatia was of the opinion that they had been more than patient with him. Certainly she and her sisters had been praying for him. Watching him now, Odelia couldn't help wondering what God had in store for Phillip. One thing she knew without doubt was that God always had a plan for His children.

She suspected that Phillip was about to find that out.

When Carissa Hopper did not return as expected that evening, Phillip was ready to climb the walls. He had scaled mountains less challenging than dealing with three kids! While little Grace beguiled everyone into getting her way, Tucker treated the mansion like his personal playground, haring off without warning. Nathan, meanwhile, remained solemn, suspicious and openly hostile, especially toward Phillip. It shouldn't have mattered, but it bothered Phillip. People usually liked him. Then again, he didn't have much experience with children. In fact, if anyone had told him that he'd have to work so hard to keep three youngsters from tearing the house down, he'd have scoffed. How Carissa Hopper had somehow managed to shelter, feed, clothe and survive this trio all alone for *years* was a mystery to him.

Hilda and Chester insisted that it wasn't like Carissa to lose track of time or forget to call, but their phone calls to her went unanswered.

Someone—Hypatia probably—alerted Phillip's baby sister, Dallas. She showed up with her short, curly, carrot-red hair held back by a wide headband. She looked a little thin to him but oddly serene. A second-grade teacher, Dallas waded right in, taking control of the children and leaving Phillip free to enjoy his dinner. When Chester came into the dining room immediately after the meal, everyone knew that something was wrong. Dressed as always in a white shirt, black tie, black slacks and black lace-up shoes, Chester looked worried, a hand smoothing over his nearly bald head.

"Carissa has been at the emergency room with her father. Now they're back home. I'm going to take some food over to them and try to convince Carissa to let the children stay here for the night."

He and Hilda lived with Hilda's sister, Carol, the aunties' maid, in the converted carriage house behind the mansion. Grace, Chester explained, could bunk with Carol for the night, leaving the small attic room, once occupied by the gardener, for the boys to share.

"Phillip can drive you over to your brother's," Odelia suggested to Chester. "I think you're too worried to go alone."

"Be glad to," Phillip said, rising from the table.

Chester didn't argue and merely nodded his head, an indication of just how worried he was.

They left a few minutes later and drove across town to an older apartment complex that had seen better days. Chester led the way to a ground-floor apartment that opened onto a depressingly bare inner courtyard. It never occurred to Phillip that he might have waited in the car until Carissa opened the door. The dismay on her face when she saw Phillip standing behind Chester left no doubt as to her thoughts on his presence there.

"Come inside," she said unenthusiastically.

The tiny vestibule opened on one side into a narrow living room and on the other into a dining room, with space large enough for only a small table and two chairs. Both rooms were strewn with toys and packed with boxes and wobbly furniture. The place seemed barely large enough for two people in Phillip's estimation, let alone five.

"How is Marshall?" Chester asked, handing over the bag filled with containers of Hilda's food.

"They wanted to keep him in the hospital," Carissa said, "but he wouldn't have it."

"All I needed was a breathing treatment," grated a raspy voice. Phillip saw a wheelchair roll into view from the dining area.

"Dad, you should be in bed."

Marshall braced his skeletal elbows on the arms of his old manual wheelchair and shook his head, wheezing with effort. "And you should be in a nice three-bedroom brick house in Dallas, but here we both are in this two-bedroom dump. Introduce me to this young man."

Carissa sighed and beckoned Phillip forward. "This is Phillip Chatam. Phillip, my father, Marshall Worth."

Phillip reached out a large, strong hand. "A pleasure to meet you, sir."

Marshall's thin, veined hand trembled. "You must be a nephew of those sisters, the triplets, that my brother works for."

"Yes, sir, I am. One of many."

Marshall waved a hand at his daughter, saying, "Sugar, put that food in the kitchen. Chester, take a load off." He pointed to a dining chair. Niece and uncle traded looks and did as instructed.

"Phillip, I'm dying," Marshall Worth said bluntly, "and this cancer's taken everything I ever had. I'll have nothing but rags and sticks to leave my daughter and grandchildren."

"Daddy," Carissa said, zipping back into the room, "that's not important."

"Chester and Hilda will do everything they can," Marshall went on, as if she hadn't even spoken, "and Carissa's a hard worker, but she barely makes enough to feed them all."

"Daddy, don't worry," Carissa pleaded.

"I can't die without knowing you'll have help," he told her tiredly.

"Daddy!"

"Don't concern yourself, sir," Phillip interjected, leaning down to place a hand on the man's rail-thin shoulder. "She won't be alone or without help. You have my word as a Chatam."

Tears filled Marshall Worth's rheumy eyes, and he nodded with relief.

"Chatams are good people, so if you say it, I believe it," he rasped.

"Believe it, sir. Your daughter and grandchildren will be fine." He smiled. "I'm told that Carissa has strong computer skills, after all."

"That she does," Marshall agreed with a chuckle. "Not much business sense, though."

"Dad!"

"But she's a good mother and a fine daughter," he added, "and she's not hard on the eyes, either."

"You slight her, sir," Phillip said, just to rankle her. "She's a rare beauty."

Her back stiffened, then she relaxed again and swept through the narrow kitchen to the other bedroom. There couldn't be another in the apartment, which meant that she probably shared it with all three of her children. Phillip realized just how blessed he was to have Chatam House as a haven in his time of trouble.

"I'm tired, brother," Marshall said, sounding it. "Help me to bed."

Chester rose and took his brother's chair by the handles, saying, "Afterward, we'll have a word of prayer together. Then I want you to eat."

"I'd like that," Marshall told him, seeming to shrink before Phillip's eyes. "Prayer and Hilda's good food. Nothing I'd like better. Goodbye, young man." Not good-night but goodbye.

"Goodbye, sir."

Phillip stood awkwardly for a moment before Carissa came back through the kitchen. "Walk me to my car?"

She didn't want to. He knew it by the way she hesitated, but she couldn't find a graceful way to decline. "All right."

As they strolled along the inner courtyard, Phillip couldn't help noting the buckling concrete of the sidewalk, the overgrown shrubbery, the disintegrating fence around the trash Dumpster and the flaking paint on the metal stairs at the corner of the building. There he paused and turned to face her, his hands tucked into his pockets.

"My aunts want to keep the children at Chatam House tonight. They can stay in the carriage house with Chester, Hilda and Carol. When your father is better tomorrow, you can pick them up and bring them home."

Carissa took a deep breath. "Well," she said, "that might work, except for one thing."

"What's that?"

"My father's not going to be better," she said softly.

Phillip couldn't resist the urge to slide an arm across her shoulders. "I'm sorry," he said.

She slowly slipped out from beneath his embrace, saying, "I'd better go pack a bag for the kids."

He was surprised that she'd given in so easily and wondered if she had done so just because she was anxious to get away from him. The thought pinched in a way he hadn't expected, but he reminded himself that her father was gravely ill. And that he had given his word to a dying man.

He would keep his word. Whether Carissa Hopper liked it or not.

But obviously, Carissa Hopper was not the woman for him. Or rather, he was not the man for her.

She needed a solid, serious, responsible man, the kind his parents had always wanted him to be. But that wasn't him, had never been Phillip Chatam. And never would be.

## *Chapter Three*

Marshall Worth lapsed into a coma during the night and was transported to the hospital the next day. The children remained at Chatam House, but with Chester staying close by them, waiting for news. Phillip tried to make good on his promise to Mr. Worth and consulted his older brother, Asher, an attorney, on Carissa's behalf. Asher promised to look into the possibility of government assistance for her and her children, then he invited Phillip—and his résumé—to lunch.

Phillip dutifully went along, though he knew what was coming. Sure enough, his brother had asked a friend with a local accounting firm if he had any openings. It made sense, after all. Phillip was good with numbers. He was good with bookkeeping. He was even good with money. It was the whole idea of being an accountant, someone else's bean counter, in a nine-to-five job that made Phillip's skin crawl. Before Asher could suggest that Phillip apply for a position, Phillip changed the subject to an article that he'd read while he'd sat in Asher's office, waiting for Asher to finish a phone call.

The article had mentioned a new smartphone app that allowed its purchasers to "test drive" possible employment fields. According to the article, a new field of reality apps allowed people to follow a day in the life of a number of professions, be it a baker, a truck driver, a plumber or a diesel mechanic. The purchase price seemed steep to Phillip, but he supposed it was worth it if it prevented a person from spending the time and money to educate him or herself for a career he or she ultimately didn't like.

Asher listened then unceremoniously informed him that Carissa made just enough money to make her ineligible for government assistance because she did not pay rent. If she could come up with the funds to get into an apartment of her own, then she could qualify for government assistance.

Phillip headed home to discuss the situation with Hilda and Chester, only to find the entire household in the front parlor with Carissa and her kids, all of whom openly wept. Tucker stood at his mother's side, literally howling.

"What's happened?" Phillip asked, already knowing.

Little Grace hopped down off her mother's lap

and ran toward him. Phillip instinctively reached down to take her up into his arms. She buried her damp face in the crook of his neck and sobbed. Tucker draped himself around his mother's neck and continued bawling, while Nathan stood stoically, tears rolling unimpeded from beneath the lenses of his glasses.

Hypatia turned a sad face to him from her usual armchair, a teacup in her hand. As always, she could have stood in for the Queen of England, her silver hair styled into a sleek roll against the back of her head, her ubiquitous pearls worn with a tailored silk suit. "Marshall Worth has slipped from this world into Paradise," she announced softly.

"Perfectly healed," Kent added in a gentle voice, his arm about Odelia on the settee.

"A brand-new body," Odelia whispered, encased in a cloud of blue chiffon.

"Without pain," Magnolia offered, patting Nathan's shoulder. She had come in without removing the yellow galoshes that she always wore when working in the gardens.

"That's what we have to remember now," Chester said in a tear-clogged voice, putting away a handkerchief.

"That's our consolation," Hilda agreed. She mopped her face with her apron, sniffed and all but wailed, "I should start dinner!" before trundling from the room. Carol followed.

Chester shook his head then said, "She isn't thinking clearly," and he went after her.

A collective sigh filled the air. A moment later, Nathan jerked away and ran from the room. Carissa calmly set Tucker onto his feet and, after a moment of uncertainty, looked to Phillip. He desperately wanted to open his arms and pull them both in, but he knew what she needed from him, so he lifted his hand to Tucker alone. The boy stumbled into his side and wrapped his arms around Phillip's waist. Phillip awkwardly patted the boy's back, and Carissa quietly went after her oldest son.

When he turned again to his aunts, they were staring as if he'd grown a second pair of arms. All but Odelia, who clasped her beringed hands beneath her double chin and, for some reason, smiled at him as if he'd hung the moon.

Carissa and the children stayed the night at Chatam House, not in the building out back where Chester and Hilda lived with Hilda's sister, Carol, but in the main house, in a three-bedroom, three-bath suite upstairs that was bigger and far finer than her father's old apartment. The Chatam sisters had suggested it, and Carissa had let herself be talked into it. Partly because she was too tired to argue, but mostly because she didn't think the children ought to go back to the apartment so soon after their grandfather's death. It seemed best to get through the next few days first.

Plucking at the black T-shirt that she'd tucked into the waist of her denim skirt, she sighed and asked, "Do you think this is all right to wear to the funeral home?"

"I think it's fine," Phillip told her, tucking a strand of hair behind her ear.

She had twisted it into a bun low on her neck, but no matter what she did, wisps escaped. Someday she would have money for a decent haircut.

"Maybe I should tie a scarf around my hair."

"No." He curled a finger beneath her chin and tilted her face up. "You look lovely just as you are."

Despite the luxury of having had a room and a bed entirely to herself, she was too tired to scold herself for enjoying the compliment. "Thank you."

"Don't worry about the kids," he told her. "I'll sit right here in the suite with them until they wake. Then I'll send them down to Hilda for breakfast."

"I've laid out their clothes."

"Don't worry."

"They can dress themselves."

"Don't worry."

"Uncle Chester says it won't take long." She bit her lip to stop its trembling.

Phillip leaned forward until his forehead touched hers. "Don't. Worry."

But how could she not? Funerals cost money, which she didn't have. Despite her best efforts, tears suddenly streamed down her face. Phillip said nothing, just gathered her loosely against him until she regained control. It would be so easy to lean on him. He had promised her father, after all, that she wouldn't be alone after his death, but she knew better than to hold him to that promise. Phillip had been pledging the support of the Chatams, not him personally. She pushed him away, grabbed her handbag and rushed out of the suite as fast as she could.

Chester, the Chatam sisters and Kent waited for her in the foyer downstairs. What a trio the sisters were, Hypatia all elegance in her silk and pearls, her silver hair expertly styled, Odelia flamboyant in eye-popping prints and oversize jewelry, her shockingly white hair curling with abandon, and Magnolia looking like a bag lady in her moth-eaten shirtwaists, her steel-gray braid hanging over her shoulder. Surprised to find them dressed to go out, their handbags dangling from their elbows, Carissa automatically protested.

"Ladies, Uncle Chester and I can take care of this."

Hypatia shook her elegant silver head. "Your uncle has been an enormous part of our lives for many years. We would never abandon him in his hour of need."

"Oh, of course."

They did far more than "not abandon" Chester, however. They made suggestions that helped trim costs without sacrificing the dignity of the service, including offering Chatam House to hold the reception at afterward. It shamed Carissa to have to ask the funeral director if he could provide a payment plan, but she had no choice.

"Oh, no, honey," Chester said, slipping an arm about her shoulders. "Hilda and I will take care of this."

"But, Uncle Chester—"

"It's been decided, Carissa. I know he was your father, but he was my brother, and he worried so about you and the children. You have enough to take care of as it is."

Carissa closed her eyes and said a silent prayer of thanks before hugging her uncle's neck. She didn't miss the small, satisfied smiles that the Chatam sisters traded or the wink that Kent gave Chester. She knew very well where Chester was getting the money to pay for this, but for once she was going to look the other way and be grateful.

* * *

The funeral service took place on Monday morning at Chester and Hilda's small church. Marshall wasn't a member, but he had often attended worship there. Dallas, Phillip's youngest sister, stepped in to watch the children at Chatam House. Carissa hoped to the very end that her sister, Lyla, would somehow get wind of the situation and arrive in time for the funeral, but that didn't happen. Thankfully, their mother didn't turn up, either. Though Alexandra had divorced their father many years ago, he had never remarried, and Alexandra was shameless enough to make a grand entrance decked out in widow's weeds and claim the spotlight. Carissa wouldn't even put it past her to bring along her current husband, a much younger man, to show off.

After the service, the Chatams hosted a reception at the mansion, catered by a local catering company to spare Hilda the trouble. Dallas brought the children in, clean and dressed. When the children became restless, Dallas took them out again, and they went off without a peep of protest.

The past few days, Carissa had let herself just drift along, going with the flow, but the moment was coming when she must again take a stand and assert her independence. Otherwise, she would wind up letting the Chatams do everything for her. She couldn't help wondering where she would find the energy to do what she must. Glancing around the large but crowded dining room, where the food had been laid out, she set aside her plate, rose to her feet and quietly slipped out of the house to the front porch. An old-fashioned bench swing hung from the east end of the porch. She kicked off her navy pumps and sat down in the middle of the swing, tucking her bare feet onto the seat beneath her.

Hanging baskets of ivy bracketed the swing, and green lawns sloped away to the street beyond. Her father would have enjoyed this place, but she didn't think he'd ever done more than drive by here. She'd seen a rose arbor on the east lawn and a towering magnolia tree on the west, as well as other trees clustered about the property. Despite the almost suffocating heat, she felt peace curl about her. She closed her eyes and let her head fall back, setting the swing in motion.

*Goodbye, Daddy. I'll miss you so much.*

She hardly noticed when she slipped into prayer, but eventually, she put her feet on the floor, leaned forward and thanked God sincerely for ending her father's pain.

*I don't know why it had to be like this. I don't understand why these things happen, but he was the best daddy he knew how to be, and I thank You for that. I wish I could have him back, but*

*I'm not selfish enough to deny him Heaven. I know he's happy and well and at peace, so just help me and everyone who loves him be happy for him and at peace with our new reality.*

She sat up straight, opening her eyes to find Phillip Chatam standing in front of her. He couldn't have looked any better, dressed in a dark olive-green suit, white shirt and tie, his dark hair gleaming, copper eyes glowing. His shoulders looked broad enough to carry the world, his hands strong enough to hold it at bay. She was tempted to throw herself into his arms and cry like a baby.

"You okay?"

She managed to nod.

"Mind if I sit?"

She did. But he was a Chatam, and she owed the Chatams. Grasping the chain holding up the swing, she slid over to give him room. He lowered himself onto the wood slats beside her and copied her previous pose, leaning forward with his forearms braced against his thighs.

"I trust that you already know this, but I've been asked to make certain that the message is delivered. My aunts want you and the children to stay on here at Chatam House indefinitely."

She was so tempted. She told herself that they could stay just one more night, but she knew that if they stayed one more night she would find an excuse to stay another and another and... She dared not start down that path. The crisis had passed. The time had come to get on with her life. She'd been here before, and she knew what she had to do. She had to get up and stand on her own two feet. Right now. So that was what she did. She put her bare feet on the gray painted wood of the porch floor and stood, turning to face him.

"I appreciate everything that the Chatams have done for us, more than I can tell you, but it's time that my children and I went home."

"Is there anything I can do to convince you to stay?"

"The Chatams have already done more than enough. We're going back to the apartment."

"Wouldn't it be easier if—"

"The sooner the better," she interrupted firmly.

Phillip bowed his head and sighed. "I'll bring the car around. We'll leave anytime you're ready."

Turning away, she snatched up her shoes and headed for the door, but once she got there, she paused and looked back. He sat just as he had, his brow furrowed, copper eyes watching her. If only he were not living here at Chatam House, she could stay without the fear that she'd do something stupid, like flirt with him or hope he'd fall for her.

Oh, it wasn't his fault. Why, he hung around here living off his elderly aunts and *still* she couldn't help liking him. Her aunt and uncle tried to make light of it, but even they wondered why he didn't go out and find a job. Even if Phillip should fall head over heels for her, what good would that do her? She needed a true partner, someone who could at least pull his own weight, but that didn't seem to matter to her heart. No more than it had with Tom, her charming rascal of a husband who had sailed through life from crisis to crisis without a care. Then she'd been left alone with three kids, a floundering business and a mortgage she couldn't pay. Well, she'd learned that lesson. The hard way. And Phillip Chatam was never going to offer to help her. She could still hear her old boyfriend explaining why they had to break up.

"It's not like any man is actually going to marry you, not with three kids in tow. One, okay. Two, maybe. But *three?* No way."

Shrugging those memories aside, she ran inside to change clothes, pack her bags and get on with this life that God had dealt her.

Unfortunately, getting away proved more difficult than she had hoped. When she came back downstairs in her jeans, she found the Chatam sisters at the door, shaking hands with departing guests. Good manners dictated that she join them, of course, which left no chance of slipping away without explanations to everyone, including her uncle and aunt, who argued that tonight of all nights she should stay.

Carissa stuck to her guns, however, and finally got the children, along with their luggage and Grace's safety seat, loaded into the Chatam's town car, Phillip behind the wheel. They waved goodbye as the car pulled away from the mansion, Grace blowing kisses and calling out to Dallas, "'Bye, bffn!"

Carissa exchanged a puzzled look with Phillip over that, but he merely shrugged, obviously having no more clue about what *bffn* meant than she did.

Despite the short drive, the closer they got to the apartment, the more subdued the children became. Carissa steeled herself and put on a brave face.

"It will be good to be home, have our own place again, huh?"

"Grandpa won't be there," Tucker pointed out softly as Phillip parked the car.

"I know," Carissa told him consolingly, "but tomorrow we'll start clearing out things, and you and Nathan can have your own room. You'll like that, won't you?"

"I guess."

She looked at Phillip and found his jaw

clenched tight. "Okay," she said brightly, hoping that he wouldn't point out how much more luxurious Chatam House was than the apartment. "Everyone lend a hand. Pop the trunk, please, Phillip."

He exited the car and did as she asked. Carissa tried to make a game of it, herding the children to the back of the sedan and assigning totes. They'd accumulated a surprising amount of stuff in their short time at Chatam House. They trudged along the walk, with Carissa in the lead and Phillip bringing up the rear of their little ragtag caravan.

When they reached the apartment door, she found a folded note taped over the keyhole. Quickly removing the small slip of paper, Carissa tucked it into a pocket before Phillip could see it, intending to read the note in private. Whatever it said, she would deal with the matter on her own. Perhaps the short letter contained nothing more than words of condolence. She didn't think so, however, especially when she slid her key into the lock and found that it wouldn't turn.

Carissa tried the key again, but the lock refused to budge. Phillip pushed forward.

"What's wrong?"

"The key doesn't work."

"You sure it's the right one?" he asked, taking it from her and trying it himself.

"Absolutely," she mumbled, slipping the note

from her pocket. While he tried to unlock the door yet again, she read the words on the paper, her heart pounding. "Um, I have to speak to the manager."

Phillip's head snapped around. "What?"

She made an attempt at a smile. "Would you wait here with the kids? I won't be long."

Pivoting on one heel, she hurried down the sidewalk and around the corner to the on-site manager's apartment. The thin, sixtysomething woman with long, graying hair and thick eyeglasses wore a series of interchangeable knit pantsuits as a kind of work uniform.

She smiled at Carissa and said bluntly, "You must have realized by now that we changed the locks."

"But why?"

"You can't stay, I'm afraid. You're not on the lease."

"Guests are allowed for six weeks at a time," Carissa pointed out. "We have at least a couple weeks left."

"Not once the legal tenant vacates the property. Legally, we could have put your belongings out yesterday, but given the circumstances, we want to be as compassionate as possible."

Panicked, Carissa tried to think through her options. "Listen, I can continue to pay the rent, if that's what you're worried about."

The manager shook her head. "This is a subsidized apartment intended for disabled tenants, and I have a lengthy waiting list of approved applicants. I'm sorry, but I can't let you and your children stay."

The breath left Carissa's lungs in a rush. She couldn't believe it. The very thing she'd feared most had just come to pass.

*Homeless.*

She and her children were now truly homeless.

Carissa felt a presence at her back and knew without looking that it was Phillip. She could only wonder how long he had been standing behind her. Biting her lip, she dug her fingernails into her palms to keep from lashing out at him. She turned and coolly said, "You were supposed to stay with the children."

"Nathan is perfectly capable of watching the other two for a few minutes," he replied before asking the apartment manager, "Could you let us into the apartment long enough to pack up some personal things tonight? If so, I'll return tomorrow to take care of everything else."

"What are you doing?" Carissa whispered under her breath.

"Just what has to be done," he answered, proving that he'd overheard everything.

"I'll get the key," the manager said, disappearing inside her apartment.

"You can't just take over," Carissa declared, trying to keep her voice low when she really wanted to yell at him.

"I'm not trying to take over. I'm just trying to help," he told her, his copper eyes so soft with compassion that she had to look away. She felt his big hands hovering near her upper arms, but thankfully, he didn't touch her. If he had, she would've crumbled into pieces. "We'll figure this out, okay? One thing is certain, though. You can't stay here."

She gulped, feeling perilously close to hysterics as the truth sank in. She and her children were actually homeless.

"Dear God," she whispered, closing her eyes. "Help me!"

## *Chapter Four*

"It's all right," Phillip said, slipping an arm about her. "Everything's going to be all right. You'll see. It's going to be a surprise for the kids, though."

*The kids.* Carissa gasped, looking up. "What are we going to tell them?"

"We'll just say that we talked it over and decided that Chatam House is the best place for everyone after all."

Carissa frowned. *We,* he'd said.

"They'll want their own things," Phillip went on, "toys, books… Nathan said something about a pillow the other day."

"He's had it since he was a baby," Carissa murmured, her mind awhirl with all that had to be done. "It's hardly even a pillow now, more like a pillowcase with some feathers in it."

"Whatever. He wants it, so he should have it with him. Don't you think?"

Carissa nodded, hardly aware of what she was doing. The utilities had to be cut off, the mail forwarded, bills paid.... What were they going to do with the furniture? The door opened behind her, and the manager briskly stepped out.

"Sorry. Phone always rings when you're busiest."

"No problem," Phillip told her. "We appreciate your cooperation."

"Oh, I'm happy to help," she said, setting off. "Wish I could do more, but it's out of my hands, you understand."

Glumly, Carissa fell in behind her. Phillip kept pace, his hand hovering in the small of Carissa's back as if he feared she would turn tail and bolt. The kids were plucking leaves out of the shrubbery and pelting one another when they got back to her father's apartment. The manager unlocked the door but didn't enter.

"I can just wait, if you won't be too long, or you can stop by when you're done, and I'll come back and lock up then."

Phillip looked to Carissa. "Give us thirty minutes."

"I'll just visit the tenant in 307, then. She always welcomes an unexpected chat. You can pop over and knock on the door when you're done."

"Thank you."

As soon as the manager left, Carissa took the

children into the living room and sat down with them, explaining that they wouldn't be staying after all.

Little Grace looked around her before commenting solemnly, "I don't want to stay, not without Grandpa."

Nathan glared at Phillip and declared, "I'm not going back with *him!*"

"We're going in our car," Carissa said huskily, too exhausted to argue with him, "back to Uncle Chester and Aunt Hilda."

Tucker rose and wandered about the room, touching this lamp and that photo. "Grandpa would want us to go," he said sadly. Phillip went over to him and patted him on the shoulder.

"Your grandfather wanted you to have a safe, comfortable home, Tucker. That's all he cared about."

"I wish he could go with us," Tucker whispered in a choked voice.

"I know," Phillip replied gently, "but his house is in Heaven now."

Tucker glanced around. "It's probably nicer than here."

"Much nicer."

"It's probably even better than Chatam House, isn't it?" Tucker said, looking up at Phillip.

Nodding, Phillip told him, "The Bible says

that where your grandpa lives now, even the streets are paved with gold."

"Oh, that's just a story," Nathan scoffed.

"I don't think so," Phillip refuted blandly. "It's written in the Bible."

"Where?"

"I'm not sure," Phillip admitted, "but we can look it up."

Nathan rolled his eyes to demonstrate his skepticism.

Carissa cleared her throat and said, "Let's figure out what we want to take with us tonight. Okay?"

"Toys?" Phillip suggested, pointing toward a box labeled in marker with that very word. Tucker brightened noticeably. "And don't forget your pillow," Phillip said to Nathan, who shoved his nose in the air then stomped off in the direction of the bedroom.

Carissa looked around her, trying to think. "I guess I need to pack the dressers."

"Are there any empty suitcases?" Phillip asked.

"Dad probably had a few." She got up and took a deep breath, bracing herself.

"Want me to look around for them?" he offered kindly.

Perhaps it was cowardly of her, but she wasn't

quite up to looking through her father's things. "Yes, thank you. Through there."

He went off toward her father's bedroom, leaving her to go to the room that she'd shared with the children these past weeks. They had managed to squeeze a full bed, which she and Grace had been sharing, and bunk beds into the small space, along with a pair of dressers. They barely had room to walk, and the arrangement made Carissa feel like a horrible failure, but she'd happily go on enduring it to have her dad back. But no. He walked on streets of gold now, as Phillip had said. She wouldn't bring him back just because she missed him, especially given how he'd suffered at the end.

Phillip arrived with several suitcases and began helping her fill them. He concentrated on the kids' things while she took care of her own. She heard Nathan snap, "Don't touch that!" and looked over to find him yanking a framed photo of him and his dad from Phillip's grasp.

"Maybe you could help with the boxes," she suggested to Phillip, her tone apologetic.

He gave her a quick smile, nodded and left the room. Nathan ducked his head, busily cramming clothes into an open bag. She decided to let the rudeness pass. They were all under a lot of stress at the moment.

When the dressers had been emptied, she got

trash bags from the kitchen and filled them with shoes and the contents of the bathroom. Then she returned to the living room to find that the children had stacked up numerous boxes that they wanted to take. Phillip was nowhere to be seen. She nixed several and was arguing with Tucker over another when Phillip wandered out of her father's room, her dad's open Bible in his big hands. He seemed to be reading even as he walked over to the threadbare sofa and lowered himself onto the edge of it.

"I found this on Marshall's bedside table," Phillip said. Flipping a red ribbon, he added, "This passage was marked." With that, Phillip began to read. "'The wall was made of jasper, and the city of pure gold, as pure as glass. The foundations of the city walls were decorated with every kind of precious stone. The twelve gates were twelve pearls. The great street of the city was of gold, as pure as transparent glass.'" As he read, the children had gathered around him, and he underlined the last part with his finger-tip so they wouldn't miss it.

"And that's where Grandpa is?" Tucker asked, looping an arm around Phillip's neck.

"I think so," Phillip said. "The Bible says all believers will spend eternity in Heaven. I tell you what—when you all get settled, we'll ask my aunts. They'll know, and they'll be glad to tell us."

Nathan said nothing, just frowned in thought. Phillip replaced the red ribbon and closed the Bible then passed it to Nathan, saying, "Why don't you hold on to this for your mom?"

Nathan seemed surprised, but he folded the Bible tightly against his chest. Phillip calmly rose and rubbed his hands together.

"Okay. Let's get this show on the road."

They packed up both vehicles in a matter of minutes. At the last moment Tucker remembered something he wanted to take with him to Chatam House, so they walked back to the apartment. Inside the tiny coat closet was his grandfather's old cap, one Tucker had worn several times while playing. Tucker smoothed the interior band before flipping the cap onto his head and nudging the bill slightly to the side. When he looked up, tears stood in his big blue eyes. He turned in a circle, looking around the place, and Carissa knew he was saying a final goodbye. Her heart stopped.

Suddenly, Tucker threw himself at Phillip, latching on to Phillip's leg. She knew just how Tucker felt. He wanted an anchor, something—someone—solid and strong to hold on to in a world that suddenly felt rudderless and bleak. Grace let out a little hiccup of a sob and lifted her arms. Without a word, Phillip picked her up and cradled her against his side. While Carissa just stood there trembling inside and yearning for some of that strength, Phillip comforted her children. Worse, she looked at Nathan and saw the same hunger in his face before he turned and stomped off. Shaken to realize that her nine-year-old had more fortitude than she did just then, Carissa brusquely ordered the other children to head to the van with their brother while she went to fetch the manager. As the woman locked up the place, Phillip renewed his promise to return the next day to empty out the apartment.

"But where am I going to put everything?" Carissa demanded as they hurried to the car.

"There are attics at Chatam House."

She shook her head. She wasn't moving in lock, stock and barrel. If she did, she might never convince herself to leave again, and the Chatam sisters were just dear enough to let her and the children stay on indefinitely.

"Well, I have a storage unit," he told her. "It's barely half-full. You can start with that, and I expect they have empty spaces for rent at the same place. We'll work something out."

She decided that she would spend the remainder of the afternoon making some calls about new apartments, and if she couldn't find something affordable, well, better that she should take advantage of *him* than his aunts.

"See you at Chatam House," he said, moving toward the town car.

Nathan put his back to the van and folded his arms. Clearly, he didn't want to go back to Chatam House—or anywhere else that left him in close proximity to Phillip. Carissa couldn't blame him. Phillip Chatam was dangerous, not just to her heart but to those of her children. What other choice did they have, though, except to return to Chatam House?

She could take her children to a motel, but even the cheapest one would drain her meager funds and delay when they could move into a suitable home of their own again. No, as badly as she wanted to avoid Phillip, she had no real choice but to accept the hospitality of the Chatams. Still…she didn't have to be right under his nose, did she?

Carissa thought about that as she drove her children back to Chatam House, and by the time they arrived, she had her argument well planned. The Chatam sisters and Kent were sitting in the formal parlor. Carissa sent the children to the sunroom then asked her aunt and uncle to come in. As soon as they arrived, Phillip explained the situation. Then Carissa spoke.

"We hate to impose on you any further, and

the truth is, we'll be much more comfortable with Uncle Chester and Aunt Hilda in the carriage house."

Odelia blinked at that. She'd traded black onyx earrings and pleated, paper-white linen trimmed in wide black edging for purple amethysts and yard upon yard of floral chiffon. Magnolia, on the other hand, wore the same dark print cotton dress that she'd worn to the funeral; she'd traded her pumps for penny loafers, however. Only Hypatia had not changed a stitch. Still wearing gray silk, matching pumps and pearls, her silver hair twisted into a sleek chignon, she looked as neat and fresh as she had at breakfast that morning.

"Well," Odelia said consideringly, "I suppose we could have Carol move into the house here to make room for you."

Carissa frowned. She hadn't meant to put anyone out of place.

"Of course, you'd still have to share a room with Grace," Hypatia said.

"And that's with Grace sleeping on the floor," Hilda put in. "There's no room for more than a half bed in either room upstairs in the carriage house."

"Oh, we have bunk beds for the boys," Carissa said quickly.

"They're attic rooms, sugar," Chester pointed

out. "The ceiling slopes too much. Bunk beds won't fit. Full beds won't fit, for that matter."

Feeling as if she'd swallowed a lead weight, Carissa bowed her head in defeat.

"The master suite is much more suitable," Odelia said brightly. "And Phillip will help you settle in. Won't you, dear?"

"I'll start unloading the car," he replied, before leaving the room.

Chester and Kent got up to follow. Magnolia leaned over to pat Carissa's hand.

"The master suite is best for all concerned," she said. "It's large and airy. You're welcome to set up your bunk beds, if you like."

Carissa nodded, hoping that wouldn't be necessary, and choked out, "Thank you. You're very kind."

"It's just practical, dear."

A sound from the hallway gave Carissa an excuse to escape. "I'd best check on the kids." Popping up, she hurried away, determined not to cry. This whole day, which she had started by burying her father, had just been one disappointment after another. It was as if God was determined to force her into close proximity with Phillip Chatam, no matter what she wanted. She couldn't make any sense of it. She couldn't even try.

Tomorrow, she decided. Tomorrow she

would take another look at her options and figure out what to do next.

As Hilda went to the kitchen for the tea tray, Odelia settled back against the cushions of the elegant antique settee and lifted her eyebrows at her sisters.

"Still think I'm making mountains out of molehills?" she asked once she could be sure they wouldn't be overheard.

Magnolia sniffed but conceded, "We have seen God move like this before."

"I'm just not certain that Phillip is cut out for a ready-made family," Hypatia said doubtfully.

"You saw the way he reacted with Grace and Tucker in the midst of their grief," Odelia argued.

"And they with him," Hypatia admitted, "but that doesn't mean there's a romance developing between Carissa and Phillip. Besides, I'm not convinced that he and Carissa could support those children."

"Mmm, and the oldest boy is none too keen on him," Magnolia pointed out.

"Nathan is none too keen on anyone or anything," Odelia said dismissively, "but he'll get over that. As for Phillip, he's an intelligent man. He'll come up with something."

"He needs to come up with a firm understanding of God's involvement in his life," Hypatia stated flatly. "And I'm sorry, Odelia, but from what I can tell, Carissa doesn't seem to like our Phillip very much."

Sighing, Odelia had to admit that it was true, though how any woman could resist Phillip's charm and masculinity, she didn't know.

"Besides, you're forgetting something else," Magnolia pointed out. She waited until she had the rapt attention of both of her sisters before bluntly saying, "Our brother."

Hypatia winced. "I hate to speak ill of a loved one, but Murdock can be a bit of a, um..."

"Snob," Odelia supplied unhappily.

Murdock and his wife, Maryanne, both dedicated doctors, had initially disapproved of their oldest son Asher's wife, Ellie, and they had actively fought the marriage of their oldest daughter, Petra, to Dale Bowen because he worked as a carpenter. They even seemed to disapprove of Phillip himself because he hadn't chosen a "premium" profession, such as law or medicine. Murdock had even once said that he'd happily settle for banking or education for his younger son, but Phillip had chosen bookkeeping instead then hadn't even gotten a job in the field.

Odelia could only imagine what Murdock and Maryanne's opinion would be of a penniless widow with three children as a daughter-in-law. She hated to think that they might even be petty enough to hold it against Carissa that her aunt and uncle had been longtime employees at Chatam House. She had once heard Maryanne refer to Chester and Hilda as servants. The very term made Odelia shudder.

On the other hand, no one could say that Murdock and Maryanne weren't dedicated parents. They had eventually accepted both Ellie and Dale, and the birth of their first grandchild, Asher and Ellie's daughter, seemed to have softened them considerably. They had both recently retired in order to spend more time with family, and the sisters had noticed a renewed interest in spiritual matters.

"What is needed here is prayer," Odelia decided.

"Indeed it is," Hypatia agreed, "for all concerned."

"Prayer," Magnolia pointed out, "is the one thing we might do that can only help and never hurt."

Odelia bowed her head. God's will was always the best answer, but she couldn't help wanting things to work out for Phillip and Carissa together. Perhaps she was just an old romantic, but it seemed like the perfect solution. Carissa needed a husband, and those children needed a father. And Phillip...so far as she could tell, Phillip just needed to grow up. Besides, next to the love of the Lord, the love between husband and wife was the most sacred and wonderful of bonds. That was a normal thing to wish for one's nephew, wasn't it?

"This is all too much," Carissa said for perhaps the fourth or fifth time. "This suite is larger than Dad's whole apartment, and moving in here is like taking over someone's house."

Phillip mentally kicked himself for mentioning that the master suite had once belonged to his grandparents and had always been considered the heart of the house.

"But this space was made for children," he pointed out, setting the last of the suitcases in the center of the sitting-room floor. "Hub Senior and Gussie were very happily married and, unlike many of their generation and wealth, they were hands-on parents. Having triplet daughters prompted them to create this suite in order to keep their infants and their nurse close by."

He went on to explain that as the other three children came along, those arrangements proved wise and useful. Even as the children got older and moved into other areas of the house, Hub and Gussie maintained the large three-bedroom suite in order to keep ailing or frightened youngsters near, especially at night.

"This is the best space for a family. Why shouldn't you use it?"

The rest of the house had undergone various renovations over the decades, the latest being Odelia and Kent's private suite.

"I don't know," she said, shaking her head. "Staying here for a few days is one thing, moving in is another."

Tired of arguing with her, he said, "So which of the aunties are you going to annoy, then, Hypatia or Odelia?"

Carissa looked at him with something akin to horror on her lovely face. The smattering of freckles across the bridge of her pert nose extended just far enough across her high cheekbones to be scarcely visible in profile, but when she turned to fully face him, as she did now, it formed a delicate mask, a gossamer veil above which her deep blue eyes frowned.

"What do you mean?"

"Well, if you decide on the small suite, you'll be next door to Hypatia's bedroom, and if you take the east suite, you'll be next to Odelia and Kent's. Of course, here, you're only next to…"

*"You,"* she finished sourly. Then she immediately looked contrite. "I'm sorry. I didn't mean that the way it sounded. We don't want to disturb anyone."

Phillip sighed. "Look, the truth is, you won't

be disturbing me or my aunts, no matter which suite you choose, but the master suite is the best for *everyone.*"

Carissa nodded. The children traded uncertain but curious looks. The interchange between Phillip and Carissa had obviously piqued their interest. Carissa noticed, as well.

"Okay. Let's get this stuff put away," she ordered. "Everybody pitch in."

By the time they worked out where to put everything, they were all exhausted, the children especially. Carissa declared that a nap was in order before dinner. Nathan made a fuss, but she insisted. Phillip wandered back into the sitting room, listening to the oddly domestic sounds of shoes hitting the floor, pillows being fluffed, hugs and kisses being traded, even the whines and complaints of tired, little voices. When Carissa returned, Phillip couldn't help smiling, thinking how sweetly rumpled she looked.

She dropped down onto the sofa. "Thanks for all your help today. I'm sorry we put you to so much trouble."

"I didn't have anything better to do," he replied lightly, waiting for her to invite him to sit.

She rubbed her hands over her face then looked up at him with some surprise, as if she was unhappy to find him still standing there. "Well, good night."

Disappointed, he said, "Good night," and he moved swiftly to the door, more hurt than he had any reason to be. Honestly, how many ways did the woman have to prove that she wasn't interested in him? She'd made it more than plain that she didn't even like him. If he had an ounce of sense, he'd keep as much distance between them as humanly possible. His resolve to do just that almost made it through the door.

Almost.

## *Chapter Five*

Yanking the door open, Phillip walked straight through it, but before he shut it closed behind him, he heard her sniff. It was the barest sound, just a catch of breath and a tiny, liquid burble. He did his best to ignore it. He tried very hard to close the door, but he just couldn't do it. Gritting his teeth, he argued with himself. From the very beginning, the woman had made it clear that something about him rubbed her the wrong way. On the other hand, she'd been under great duress from the moment he'd met her. And today, she'd buried her father. As if to underscore that, she made a soft, gasping sound, and he lost the fight.

Covering the distance to the sofa in three long strides, he dropped down next to her and pulled her into his arms without a word. She dissolved, plastering herself against him to muffle the sobs that she'd tried so hard to keep hidden. As he folded her close, he felt an odd sense of purpose even amid her emotional storm. She might stab him again with that sharp tongue of hers before he finally went on his way, but he didn't much mind, not really. He rather enjoyed her independent, outspoken nature. At this very moment, he didn't think he'd much mind if she ripped him to shreds and handed him the pieces in a gunnysack.

Phillip put his hand in Carissa's hair. It felt like the softest silk. Stroking it tenderly, he crooned comforting sounds as Carissa wept.

"Shhh, shhh. It's all right, sweetheart. Don't cry."

"Nothing's gone right," she wailed in a tiny voice.

"I know it seems that way, but you're okay."

"I've failed at everything I've ever done."

"How can you say that with those three amazing kids?" he asked, astounded.

"I've failed them at every turn," she insisted. "I can't even provide a proper home for them."

"What do you call this?"

"Charity!"

"Only until you earn enough money to get into your own place."

"With what? Telephone sales?" she scoffed. "I haven't worked in days."

"You just buried your father. Besides, you

can't work all the time. Give yourself a break, will you?"

"You don't understand," she said, putting some distance between them. "I was living with my father because I lost our home when my business failed."

Her father had alluded to something like that, so Phillip wasn't surprised.

"At least you *had* your own business," he said. "That's more than I've ever had. What kind of business was it?"

She shook her head, but then explained. "Proprietary software. You know, personalized code, one-of-a-kind stuff for specialized businesses."

"Oh. I didn't realize there was a need for that kind of thing."

"Obviously not a great need," she muttered, laying her head back onto his shoulder.

Phillip pondered that for a moment. "You're talking about actually creating computer programs from scratch."

She tilted her head, giving him an odd look. "They all use the same language. Only the platforms are different."

Widening his eyes, he grinned. "O-kay."

Warming to the subject, she started to explain in detail. "The code is in the pattern. These days you just have to put in the commands—"

He held up a hand. "Don't bother. It's all Greek to me."

Suddenly Grace appeared in the doorway to the little hall that opened off the sitting room and led to the suite's two smaller bedrooms. "Mommy," she said, rubbing her eyes with both fists, "where's the air fixer? I'm cold."

Carissa bolted upright, shrugging off Phillip's arm in one frantic movement. "Uh. The air..."

"The thermostat is on that wall," Phillip said, pointing, "but I've found that in this big old house it's sometimes best just to close the vents in certain rooms. I'll take care of it."

"No, no," Carissa insisted, beating him to a standing position. "We're fine. You can go now."

Her pinkened cheeks clearly demonstrated her embarrassment at having been caught sitting with his arm around her, and now she was none-too-subtly dismissing him. Again. He took his time getting to his feet just to let her know that he didn't appreciate being sent away like a neighbor kid who had overstayed his welcome. Her hands fluttering like hummingbirds, Carissa went to escort Grace back to bed, but before she could reach her daughter, Grace ran straight for Phillip. As the girl raised her little arms, Phillip realized that she was about to launch herself. He didn't know whether to hold her off or pretend he didn't understand what she wanted. In the end, he simply caught her and swung her up into his arms.

Grace wrapped herself around him, her arms, legs and wiry little body clutching him. "You forgot my night-night hug," she informed him, squeezing with all her might.

He laughed, hugging her back. "Here's a super-duper one to make up for it."

"Super-duper!" she crowed, all but throttling him.

Carissa started forward, an anxious look on her face. Phillip met her halfway and handed off Grace with a smile and a pat for the girl's soft red head. Turning, he left as quickly as he could then. His heart felt too big for his chest, and he could have sworn that a tiny fist clutched a corner of it.

But what really shook him to the core was how right it had felt to hold Carissa Hopper in his arms, and how easily her problems seemed to become his problems. He'd called her sweetheart, of all things.

Maybe she hadn't noticed. Suddenly, he didn't want to face her across the dinner table, not after Grace had caught them all but embracing on the couch. He wondered what excuse he might give the aunties for going out and even went so far as to call his older brother, Asher, to see if he and Ellie had plans for the evening. They did, so Phillip called his younger sister Petra next, but it was her and Dale's bowling night. In sheer desperation, he telephoned his baby sister Dallas and offered to treat her to a meal at one of her favorite restaurants in thanks for her help with the kids that morning. She readily accepted, and though he had misgivings, Phillip preferred to risk Dallas's infamous prying than take a chance on sitting down to dinner with Carissa.

He need not have worried. Over their steaks, Dallas chatted about the children, saying that Tucker viewed him, Phillip, as something of a hero, which Phillip found flattering but suspect, and that Grace adored him, which made Phillip smile. He felt a certain fondness for the little girl himself. Dallas admitted that Nathan resented Phillip terribly but advised that the boy would eventually come around. To her credit, Dallas said nothing about Carissa, neither did she ask any questions about a possible relationship between him and Carissa.

Instead, he and his sister discussed his nonexistent job search and the continuing-education course she was taking over the summer. She warned him that their newly retired parents were going to be spending more time in Buffalo Creek than ever before.

"What makes you think so?"

Dallas smiled. “Asher’s daughter, Marie Ella, of course.”

Phillip frowned. “What does our niece have to do with it?”

“She’s their first grandchild, and the older she gets, the more difficult it seems to be for them to stay away,” Dallas answered wryly.

Phillip was horrified. “Surely, you aren’t saying you think they’ll move here from Waco!”

Laughing, Dallas said, “Stranger things have happened. But it’s only sixty miles. I think they might content themselves with driving up a couple times a week.”

“We can only pray,” Phillip muttered, and Dallas laughed again.

Phillip loved his parents, but the last thing he needed was his father advising him on career choices and his mother pushing him to settle down.

Dallas changed the subject then, announcing that she was dating someone new. In the next breath, she stated calmly that she sensed it wasn’t going anywhere, though she didn’t know why. She seemed sad about that but not overly disturbed. Phillip understood all too well. He’d never had a relationship that lasted longer than six months, and the very thought of it made him sad.

What was going on with him and Carissa?

He constantly felt the need to know what she was doing and that she was well, and he didn't like that.

He didn't like it at all.

Thanks to the dumbwaiter in the wall on the landing just outside the door to the master suite, Carissa and the children were able to enjoy a private dinner that evening. Carissa kept things low-key afterward by digging out a board game. After making certain that Nathan and Tucker each won a game and Grace came in second, Carissa allowed the children to watch some TV before starting the process of baths and bedtime stories. This necessitated some unpacking.

However, the children didn't appear inclined to hurry the process. They had lived with unpacked boxes for a long time already at their grandfather's; that apparently felt normal to them. At the same time, they seemed quite comfortable in their rooms, though Nathan complained about having to share a queen-sized bed with his brother.

"The Chatam ladies said we could bring in the bunk beds if you want," Carissa ventured carefully, much to Tucker's delight.

"I want a princess bed like yours!" Grace declared, running into the room in a towel while trailing her nightgown behind her. She had been in love with the large sleigh bed in the master bedroom since she'd first laid eyes on it. A genuine antique, the thing scared Carissa. What if she accidentally damaged it? She didn't even want to know what something like that was worth.

"The bed you're sleeping in is just fine," Carissa said, taking the towel to dry her daughter's back before pulling the nightgown over her head and helping her slip her arms through the sleeves. Carissa patted the mattress of the boys' bed, saying, "Hop up so we can read."

"No, I want to read in the princess bed," Grace persisted.

Before Carissa could insist that they all pile onto the bed in the boys' room, Tucker let out a yip and raced out into the short hallway, a giggling Grace on his heels. Nathan rolled his eyes but followed, the chosen book under his arm. Sighing, Carissa went after them. They had made it halfway across the sitting room when a knock came from the outer door of the suite, freezing them all in their tracks. Carissa's breath caught. Was that Phillip come to say good-night? If so, the children would be thrilled—unfortunately, so would she.

She remembered him crooning the word *sweetheart* to her earlier that evening when she'd fallen apart in his arms. She was sure he hadn't meant it romantically, but it had been so long since anyone had said anything even remotely romantic to her that she couldn't stop thinking about it.

"Come in."

Disappointment hit Carissa when Odelia Chatam Monroe's frothy white hair appeared around the edge of the door.

"Are we inconveniencing you?"

"Not at all. You're always welcome."

She opened the door and came in, her lime-green caftan fluttering like gigantic butterfly wings. Phillip entered right behind her. Carissa's heart fluttered at the sight of him. Oh, she wished he'd stay away—and was extremely glad he wouldn't, whatever his reasons. She couldn't prevent a small smile of greeting.

He seemed to relax but remained silent as Odelia asked kindly, "How are you bearing up?"

Tucker screwed up his face. "Bearing up?"

"She wants to know how you're doing," Phillip explained with a wink.

"It's been a long, difficult day," Odelia said, "with your grandfather's funeral this morning and you not being able to go back to his apartment."

To everyone's surprise, Grace suddenly burst into tears, wailing, "I want Grandpa!"

"Oh, darling," Odelia crooned, even as Carissa went down on one knee to pull Grace into her arms.

Clearly embarrassed, Nathan poked his sister in the shoulder and hissed, "Shut it! He was always old and sick and about to die."

"Nathan!" Carissa scolded.

"We all knew it," Nathan insisted.

"You're right," Phillip said, "but it's still sad."

Nathan folded his arms and looked down.

"Can we stay here now?" Tucker wanted to know, clearly concerned.

"For a while," Carissa said evasively.

"How long?" Nathan demanded.

"It doesn't matter," she told him. "I expect all of you to be on your very best behavior, especially while I work."

Nathan scowled, and Tucker frowned.

"Boys," she prompted. "I want your word that you'll be on your best behavior. Otherwise, we'll have to find someplace else to stay. Do you hear?"

Nathan nodded reluctantly, while Tucker whispered, "Yes, Mom."

Carissa gave Grace a squeeze. "That goes for you, too, young lady."

Grace made a solemn face and nodded, then she looked at Phillip and broke into a wide smile, even as her tears sparkled on her cheeks. "I'll be good," she said. "I promise."

Phillip chuckled. "I'm sure you will."

Smiling, Carissa dried her daughter's face with her fingertips, as Odelia moved to the sofa and sat down, gathering the boys to her.

"Perhaps, after a day like today, we should all have a word of prayer together."

"Oh. Of course," Carissa said, bowing her head.

She kept her eyes open, however, and saw that her children glanced at each other in some confusion. Had it been so long since they'd prayed together outside of church or around the dinner table? She promised herself that she would do better in the future. From now on, they would pray together every night. Resisting the urge to glance at Phillip, she listened as Odelia began to pray aloud, thanking God that Marshall was now happy and well in Heaven. She praised God for making it possible for her and her family to have the Hoppers as their guests and made it clear that they were welcome to stay as long as they liked. Finally, she asked that God's will be done in all their lives.

After the prayer, Carissa felt better, and her children seemed to, as well. Even Nathan seemed more relaxed. As Phillip escorted Odelia to the door, Carissa thought that if he were not in the house, the situation would be very nearly perfect. Then she wouldn't have to worry about this hopeless attraction and these unwieldy emotions leading her into something that could only leave her—and her children—brokenhearted.

Odelia took her leave of them, saying that breakfast would be served in the sunroom at eight in the morning. Carissa thanked her and waited for Phillip to go, as well, but he lingered a moment longer.

"Do you have everything you need?"

"Yes. Everything."

"Dallas will come by to stay with the kids in the morning."

She made an exasperated sound. "You can be very high-handed, you know. I'm used to managing my own children, thank you."

"Okay," he said. "I'll tell her to forget it. Don't get your feathers ruffled. I just thought that since we were going to be busy emptying the apartment…"

Carissa ached to tell him that she could take care of the apartment on her own, too, but she knew the truth. She couldn't move furniture by herself, and she couldn't ask Chester to take off work to help her when Phillip, a much younger man with free time, had already volunteered.

"Yes. Thank you."

He inclined his head. "See you at breakfast, then."

She managed a smile and nodded, wondering if it was possible to choke on one's pride. That thought plagued her for some time, but despite some tossing and turning, she slipped off to sleep and, after a surprisingly restful night, hit the ground running on Tuesday morning.

The first item on her to-do list was to cancel the phone at her dad's apartment and get a private telephone installed in the suite. That required nearly an hour of her time to arrange. Phillip showed up during breakfast in the sunroom. He wore cargo pants, a simple T-shirt and lace-up boots. A bandanna and a pair of gloves had been tucked into various pockets.

Carissa did her best to ignore him while she talked to the telephone company on her cell phone. Tucker and Grace ignored *her* while she snapped her fingers at them as they tried to use Phillip as a jungle gym. Somehow, he still managed to help himself to bacon, eggs, toast, orange juice and coffee. Then he cleaned his plate, tickled Grace and held off Tucker all at the same time. After that, Phillip coaxed the younger kids into eating their own meals, all before Carissa got off the phone. Throughout, Nathan glared sullenly and picked at his food until he finally managed to clean the plate.

Carissa gulped down her cold coffee and rose to leave, anxious about emptying the apartment, but Phillip wouldn't budge until he'd slapped some scrambled eggs and bacon between two pieces of toast, wrapped the resulting sandwich in a paper napkin and thrust it into her hands.

"Go," he said, then, "Eat on the way."

Biting her tongue rather than the sandwich, she headed for the door. The children quickly followed behind her.

"Whoa, whoa, whoa," Phillip barked, bringing everyone to a halt. "Where are they going?" He pointed to the children.

"With us," she answered, frowning. "They can help."

He lifted a hand to the back of his neck. After a moment, he waved a hand. "Fine. Go. I'm right behind you. Just have to stop off and trade my car for a truck."

Sandwich in hand, Carissa herded the children into the minivan and set off for the apartment. By the time Phillip arrived, she'd eaten and gotten the key, as well as a number of empty boxes, from the manager. Thankfully, the manager told her not to worry about cleaning the place after it was emptied, saying that a special cleaning crew would have to be brought in anyway. Carissa unlocked the apartment so she and the children could begin loading the van.

Phillip had borrowed a pickup truck from his brother-in-law, Dale, who was a carpenter, which made their job much easier. It also helped that most of her stuff was already boxed. Despite a fistfight between Tucker and Nathan, Grace falling and skinning her elbow, a broken lamp and a shattered picture frame glass, they made progress. In fact, they had moved a full load, shifted around Phillip's few things inside the hot metal storage space to make room, unloaded Carissa's boxes and were stacking them when Dallas arrived at the storage unit just before lunchtime.

Looking enviously at the neat redhead's cool white capris and matching tank top worn beneath a turquoise gauze shirt, Carissa pushed her lank, plain brown hair out of her eyes and tried not to slouch in her baggy cutoffs and gray T-shirt.

"Have you come to help us move?" Carissa asked.

"In this sweltering heat?" Dallas returned, pushing her white sunglasses farther up her nose with a perfectly manicured fingertip. "Actually, I thought I'd go swimming at Chatam House." She pulled the shades down to look over them at the children. "Want to come?"

Both Tucker and Grace started jumping up and down, and even Nathan yelled, "Yes!"

Phillip mopped his sweaty face with the bandanna and lifted his eyebrows at Carissa. It was only going to get hotter out here, of course, and things would go much more smoothly without the children underfoot. Still, her self-respect warred with her common sense and her concern for her children. In the end, of course, her dignity bowed to logic.

"Do you think you can manage all three of them in the pool by yourself?"

"Not only am I a schoolteacher," Dallas reminded her, "I'm also an excellent swimmer, lifeguard certified."

"Please, Mom!" Tucker wheedled.

"I'll stay with them until the two of you return, no matter how late," Dallas promised.

"We've already taken such advantage of you," Carissa argued. "You were with them for hours yesterday."

"For which I was amply rewarded with a steak dinner," Dallas replied, smiling at Phillip.

"You were?" Carissa said, her sharp gaze piercing Phillip.

He spread his hands. "So sue me. I wanted steak, and I don't like eating alone." He looked at his sister. "Will you talk to her, please?"

Dallas smiled at Carissa. "Look, I'd much rather take your children swimming than help you move your stuff. So, which is it? Do you listen to me whine and complain all afternoon, or do I get your kids out of this awful heat?"

Carissa gave in. "Thank you so much for taking the children swimming."

Dallas beamed, and the children cheered. Phillip stepped forward to kiss his sister's cheek.

"I'll take Grace's safety seat from the van, if that's all right," Dallas said brightly.

"Whatever you need," Carissa said, handing over the key.

"Let's go, bffn!" Grace cried, tugging on Dallas's arm.

Carissa had forgotten that *bffn* thing. She shared a glance with Phillip, who shook his head and shrugged.

"What is that?" she asked Dallas, but the other woman just waved it away as she turned the children toward the front of the storage unit.

"Oh, it's nothing. Be right back."

Dallas and the children disappeared, chattering happily among themselves.

Carissa turned to Phillip. "You engineered this, didn't you?"

He reached around for another box and stacked it. "Listen," he said, "contrary to public opinion, I do understand pride. But *you* need to accept friendship."

Carissa bit her lip and nodded.

"Besides," he went on, "it's way too hot for the kids out here."

He was right, of course. "I know. So, thank you. Again. Now, let's get to it."

Chuckling, he went to work, pausing only to

toss his sister a smile when she returned the van key to Carissa.

"Keep them out of everyone's way, will you?" Carissa instructed urgently as the vibrant redhead again disappeared from sight.

"Don't worry!" Dallas called.

"Relax," Phillip counseled. "Dallas is great with children. She likes them, and they like her. I think even Nathan likes her."

"Yes, well," Carissa admitted, embarrassed. "It's only men who I—" She swallowed what she'd been about to say, that it was only attractive men that Nathan disliked, men who could possibly replace his late father.

Phillip stopped what he was doing, a thoughtful expression on his too-handsome face, then continued working, all the while studiously avoiding her gaze. Carissa did likewise. Whatever the reason for his lack of employment, it wasn't because he was afraid to work. Far from it.

She didn't understand him. She didn't even want to understand him. She didn't want to get that close to him. But he definitely wasn't the lazy bum she'd tried to convince herself he was. Not that it mattered. For whatever else he was, she knew this much about him:

Phillip Chatam was heartbreak waiting to happen.

# *Chapter Six*

Before long, Phillip had all the boxes neatly stacked, and still a good deal of room remained inside the storage unit.

"I think we might just be able to get everything in here," Carissa said. "Your share of the monthly rent ought to be minimal after this."

"My share of the monthly rent is already zero," Phillip told her. "I paid for six months in advance less than six weeks ago."

"And you're not going to let me pay you anything for my use of the space, are you?"

"Nope. What would be the point in that? It would just be sitting there empty if you weren't using it."

She threw up her hands, torn between gratitude and irritation. She was finding it increasingly difficult to be irritated with him, however.

"Why did you lease such a large unit, anyway?" she asked as they pulled down the roll-up door and Phillip replaced the padlock.

"I intended to start accumulating some things so I could set up housekeeping in my own place. I thought it would be easier to keep it here until I decided where I wanted to live than to cart it up to the attic at Chatam House. That's why I didn't just stash my climbing junk with the aunties to begin with."

"You were serious about climbing mountains, then?"

"Yep. That was my last job."

"I see. And you quit because?"

"I quit because after some friends of mine were killed in an accident, I no longer felt I could give the job my best efforts."

"Of course. Makes sense."

"It would make better sense if I'd had another job to go to."

"Yeah, there is that. Speaking of which, I need to get this done so I can get back to mine."

"Let's go."

She walked to her van and got inside. He followed her in the pickup truck back to the apartment, where she went through her father's belongings, boxing up what could be put in storage, setting aside what needed to go to Chatam House and throwing away or stacking for donation everything else. Meanwhile, Phillip broke down the beds, emptied the bookshelves and started hauling out what was ready to go.

Hilda sent Chester over with lunch. Before returning to Chatam House, Chester helped Phillip move a load of furniture to the storage unit, told them to call when they were ready for dinner and reported that the children had napped after swimming and were looking forward to a botany lesson that Dallas had promised them.

"Botany?" Carissa asked as the door closed behind her uncle.

Phillip smiled. "That's what we called it when we went tramping around with Aunt Mags as children. Dallas is going to show them all the shady, secret places on the estate where pirates bury treasure and enchanted princesses hide. The thing is, you have to learn the parts of the plants and their Latin names to hear the secrets."

"Sounds wonderful."

"It is. They'll love it."

"Better that than this," Carissa said softly, glancing around at her father's things.

They ate lunch bit by bit over the course of the afternoon as they worked. More than once, Carissa found herself reduced to tears. She also found Phillip right beside her, ready to distract or comfort her. One time, he had a fresh tissue to offer; another time, he handed her a glass of cool water. Sometimes, he would only pat her silently on the shoulder or squeeze her fingers. Once, he sat down next to her on the floor, held out a container of strawberries that Hilda had sent and bumped his shoulder against hers until she laughed and began to eat. When she came across a stack of greeting cards from her and her sister that their dad had saved over the years, Phillip listened as she complained bitterly about her sister, Lyla. Then Phillip held Carissa as she wept because she knew that Lyla's absence and long silence must have hurt their dad.

"He's beyond that now," Phillip reminded her. "Perhaps he even understands it."

"Do you really think so?"

"I honestly don't know," Phillip admitted, "but I've always heard that whatever we need to be happy is in Heaven, so if your father needs that..."

She pulled away, drying her eyes on a paper napkin. "It occurs to me that I haven't read my Bible as much as I ought to."

"Hmm. That makes two of us."

"I'm not sure I really know where to start," Carissa admitted.

"Me, either," Phillip said, "but I know who does."

"Your aunts." Smiling, he nodded.

"It's something to think about. But first..." Phillip waved a hand, indicating the apartment.

Sighing, Carissa turned back to her task.

They wound up skipping dinner. It wasn't planned. They just kept pushing to finish, and by the time they had emptied the apartment, it was past nine o'clock. They loaded her van with the items that she wanted to keep with her and drove them over to Chatam House, where Chester promised to unload them. Then, exhausted, dirty and famished, they grabbed burgers and fries on their last trip to the storage unit and ate them while sitting on the tailgate of the truck with the door lifted on the unit and the inside light on.

"Pathetic, isn't it?" she remarked after scarfing down half her burger.

"What?"

She jerked her head at the packed unit. "My father and I together couldn't even fill one storage unit with our belongings."

"What about me?" Phillip said. "Most of what I have in there is climbing gear that I'll probably never use again. The sum total of my worldly goods is a car, some clothes, two sets of bed linens, a box of dishes, a few books, the aforementioned climbing gear and…" He fished his cell phone from a pocket. "This. I travel light."

"You don't have three children to provide for, entertain and try to make comfortable."

"And it's a good thing. Right now, I can't provide for, entertain or make *myself* comfortable."

"You're doing as well as I am."

He shook his head. "No, I'm not. At least you have a family, and you've done a good job. You sure try hard."

She couldn't help being pleased by his praise. "Thanks, but it was lots easier before Tom died. Oh, don't get me wrong. He was no businessman. Frankly, he didn't always work as hard as I wished he would or take problems as seriously as he should have, but he always made me feel that everything would work out and...when you come right down to it, two are better than one."

Phillip nodded his understanding and asked, "How did you meet him?"

"He was my high school sweetheart. We married as soon as I graduated, while he was still in college. I worked to put him through, and as soon as he got a good-paying job, we started our family. I was twenty-three when Nathan was born, and I didn't think life could get any better. Turned out I was right. Tom started his own business while I was pregnant with Tucker, and the money got tight right away. Oh, it was still great, but I worried. I wanted a girl, though, and Tom was a more-the-merrier kind of guy, so we had another baby." Carissa misted up, remembering. "Grace was so perfect, a sweet little doll.

Tom just held her and cooed at her for hours on end. And she has no memory of him. None. After Tom died, Nathan picked her up and wouldn't put her down. I had to make him let go of her so she would sleep."

"He tried to step into his father's shoes at the very beginning, then."

"Yes."

"How old was he?"

"Five and a half."

Phillip blew out a breath, taking that in fully. She waited patiently until Phillip spoke again.

"Do you mind if I ask exactly how Tom died?"

She had expected the question. Eventually, it always came to this. "Tom was a self-trained mechanic. He was doing a side job to pick up extra money, helping a friend restore an old vehicle. It fell on him while he was working beneath it. We figure he accidentally kicked one of the jacks holding it up."

"I see."

"Couldn't have happened at a worse time," she went on numbly. "The business was faltering. He'd borrowed against the equity in the house, cashed in his life insurance, emptied the 401(k). I did my best to carry on." She shook her head. "I worked other jobs, too, but eventually I lost it all."

Phillip jumped off the back of the truck. "I'm

amazed you held out so long! In this economy, I can't believe you could find a job that pays enough to feed your children, let alone house them."

"I do have some skill," she muttered.

"*I* have some skill," he retorted. "You have pure grit." He clapped a hand to the back of his neck, admitting, "You make me ashamed of myself."

"What?"

"I have three degrees. Did you know that?"

"What?" she repeated stupidly, uncertain where he was going with this.

"I have three degrees!" he all but shouted. "And do you know why I don't have a job?"

"No."

"Because I don't want one, that's why, not a normal, nine-to-five kind of job, anyway. I can't bear to be bored, you see. I want the new, the exciting, the different. Why else would I climb mountains?"

"I don't know," she admitted. "I never thought about it."

"Of course not," he retorted. "Why would you? You're too busy doing what you have to do. Me, I've always done just what I've wanted to do." He shook his head and pointed at the stuff in the bed of the truck. "Let's finish this. I want a shower and a shave and a cool bed, and in case you haven't noticed, I usually get what I want."

Carissa could have pointed out that he'd worked hard for no reason other than kindness that day, but she sensed that nothing she could say would be welcome at that moment. Besides, she was trying not to get too close to him. Wasn't she?

Confused, she threw away the trash from their meal and went to work. Later, she would think about what he'd said. Or perhaps not. Perhaps it would be safer *not* to think about it. Now, if only she could somehow stop.

Her strength amazed him. Phillip thought about all that she'd told him, and somewhere along the way, he faced an ugly fact about himself: what she'd been through would have broken him. To have a spouse die because of a foolish accident, then to be left in debt with nothing to fall back on while trying to care for three young children? It boggled his mind. He couldn't imagine how she'd managed to hold on as long as she had. Marshall had said that she was a poor businesswoman, but what else could she have done? Maybe her father thought she should have cut her losses sooner. All Phillip knew was that he was done moping and drifting and waiting for something to happen.

His parents were right. He'd been irresponsible, self-indulgent, immature. He'd played at life, and he didn't know how to stop. The deaths of his friends should have shaken some sense into him, but while he felt sick about what had happened, it hadn't changed anything for him, not like Tom Hopper's loss had impacted Carissa and her children. Tom Hopper was responsible for Carissa's situation. He'd left her in a terrible mess. Yet, she spoke of him with such…love.

The sound of it in her voice turned Phillip inside out, and that worried him. In an odd way, it also gave him a feeling of hope and purpose. The whole thing was a conundrum that kept him arguing with himself as they unloaded the truck one last time then climbed into the cab for the drive back to Chatam House.

Exhausted, Carissa dropped off to sleep almost immediately. Relieved, Phillip let her snooze. His thoughts were uncomfortable enough without those big, deep blue eyes asking silent questions of him.

Her old van sat in front of the great mansion when they arrived. It looked broken and tired, much like the lady herself at the moment. She slumped on the bench seat across from Phillip.

Dallas's little coupe was parked in front of the rusty old van, which told Phillip that his sister was as good as her word. He would owe her big-time for this one, and he didn't mind a bit. However, all he wanted was to put an end to this interminable day.

He parked the truck behind Carissa's van, released his seat belt to slide over and reached out to gently shake Carissa by the shoulder. She let out a soft little snore that pulled a smile from him. Did the woman *have* to be so endearing? Even her fits of temper made him want to hug her.

"Time to wake up, sleepyhead."

She shifted toward him, mumbling, "Mmm, five more minutes."

He released her seat belt and slid an arm across her shoulders to steady her, saying with a chuckle, "It's not morning yet, silly girl."

She sighed deeply. "Oh, good. I'm too tired."

To his surprise, she snuggled close, knocking the clip out of her hair. It tumbled down in a twisted rope far longer than he'd realized it would be. He lifted a hand to touch its silky softness, and she slid her arms around his neck.

"Mmm," she whispered, "I've missed this."

Phillip froze, fearing that she was dreaming of her husband, but when she lifted her chin and kissed him, he felt utterly powerless to resist her.

"Carissa?" he asked against her lips.

Her lashes fluttered, and for an instant, her gaze seemed to lock with his. Then her lids shuttered down again, and she stretched upward, propelling herself into the kiss. Phillip folded her close and kissed her as he'd wanted to for some time, if he was to be honest with himself.

Oh, she was sweet, a perfect fit in his arms. He'd known it would be this way, of course. From the moment he'd first laid eyes on her, he'd known, deep down, that this woman would fit into his arms, into his heart, as no one ever had.

He still couldn't figure out how she could ever fit into his life or vice versa. What on earth would he do with a woman like her, let alone her kids? He was less suitable husband and father material than the man who had left her in this fix. But that didn't keep him from kissing her as if she belonged to him.

Realizing belatedly that his heavy beard must be scratching her delicate skin, that he probably smelled like a goat, that he hadn't told her how beautiful she was, or how unworthy he felt to be holding her like this, he began preparing himself to pull back. First, he mentally put together an apology for taking advantage of her. She had been sleeping and no doubt dreaming of her late husband. He shouldn't have kissed her back. If she hadn't reached for him, looking so sweet, with her sleepy eyes and soft smile…

Suddenly, she shoved away, gasping, an expression of horror on her face.

"Oh, no!"

He'd waited too long. If he'd had to kiss her, why hadn't he called a halt to it a little earlier?

"It's not your fault," he began, but she'd already yanked open the door and run out of the truck. "Carissa, please."

He jumped out and followed her up the walkway, across the porch and through the front door, which she'd left wide open. By the time Phillip got inside, she'd torn past two of the aunties, Hypatia and Magnolia, and was literally sprinting up the staircase.

"Goodness!" Hypatia exclaimed, looking down at him in alarm. "Is everything all right?"

Sick at heart, Phillip closed the front door. What now? Go after her? Apologize? Explain? He couldn't even explain what had just happened to himself, let alone to Carissa. Or the aunts. His heart dropped into his stomach, which promptly turned over. Gulping, he made himself face the aunties, only to find that Dallas had appeared on the stairway above them.

"What's wrong with Carissa?"

He started trudging up the stairs. Weary words tumbled out of his mouth, all true, so far as they went. "She's overtired. And grieving. It's been a long, difficult day. Going through her father's things wasn't easy for her."

"The poor thing," Magnolia said. Hypatia merely looked thoughtful.

"She seemed very anxious to look in on the children," Dallas reported.

Phillip paused beside her on the stairs, suddenly so tired that he could drop where he stood. "I can't thank you enough for today, sis. Having the kids there to go through their grandfather's things was almost more than any of them could bear, I think."

Dallas smiled and patted his arm. "I'm glad I could help."

"I'd hug you, but I'm too filthy."

Chuckling, she headed down the stairs. "I'll take a rain check."

"Good thinking." He nodded to his aunts. "Now, if you'll excuse me, I'm going to shower and go to bed."

Dallas bade him a good night, as did Hypatia and Magnolia. He went to his room and cleaned up. He should have known that Odelia would stop in as soon as he was done with his shower. Feeling defeated and wary, he dressed and went out to speak to her.

Of all the aunties, she was the one he had always found it most difficult to face as a misbehaving boy. Perhaps she wasn't the brightest of the triplets, but Odelia radiated an innocence and goodness that endeared her to the whole family.

Not for anything in the world would he ever tell her how he had taken advantage of a woman—or how deeply it had hurt to see Carissa's horror when she had realized just who she had been kissing.

What a heavy beard her nephew had, Odelia mused. She found it a very manly trait. Her sisters found his scruff untidy, but they were less worldly than she was. She, after all, was a *wife*. Besides, she'd always harbored a secret appreciation for a rugged male, and this particular nephew of hers was nothing if not valiant.

Smiling to herself, she watched Phillip towel his thick, dark hair then smooth it with his hands. She saw his exhaustion, felt his impatience and sensed a good deal more.

"I gather that you've had a trying day, Phillip dear."

He shrugged and reached inside the bathroom to hang the towel. "Tougher for Carissa than me."

Odelia struggled to contain her smile. So, he was more concerned for Carissa than himself, was he? "How is Carissa now? I understand that she seemed upset when she came in tonight."

Phillip turned away, but not before Odelia caught the troubled expression on his face. "I, um, haven't talked to her since we got back.

I thought I'd give her some time. She's been through so much. Do you know about her sister?"

"I do," Odelia said. "It's no secret."

Her parents had gone through an ugly divorce, after which Carissa had stayed with her dad. Lyla, who was younger, had bounced back and forth from her mother to her father, always feeling that she was being made to choose between them, until she'd run away at sixteen.

"It's been nine years," Phillip confirmed, "and in all that time, there have apparently been only a few cards, none with return addresses. Lyla probably doesn't even know that her father is dead."

Odelia sighed. "How sad."

"And that's just the beginning," Phillip went on, telling his aunt how Carissa's husband had died, leaving her and the children in a financial fix. Odelia clucked her tongue. "And now she's essentially homeless."

"Well, she is not without friends or family," Odelia pointed out. "Be sure she knows you're praying for her."

He gave her a limp smile. "I don't think that would mean much to her, Aunt Odelia, and I'm not sure God wants to hear from me anyway."

Her jaw dropped. Not want to hear from him? "God always wants to hear from His children."

"But if God is omniscient, He already knows

what we need," Phillip argued. "He doesn't need to hear us bleating about it."

"*If?* Of course He knows what we need. That doesn't mean our prayers don't matter to Him."

Phillip blinked. "Still, He must value your prayers more than mine. I mean, as Christians go, I'm barely average."

"Do you really think that's what matters? That God chooses favorites and only listens to them? Tell me, whose communication would Marshall have most coveted? Carissa, who stayed close to him, or Lyla?"

Phillip reasoned aloud, "Well, he'd have valued Carissa's words because she was so good to be there for him. She stuck by him when Lyla didn't, so he'd naturally have valued Carissa's presence and conversation. But he'd have been thrilled to hear from Lyla because she was his daughter, too, and he had to miss her, so..." Shamefaced, Phillip blushed. "Both. He'd have coveted communication from both of them, which means that God must value communication from His wayward children as much as His obedient children."

Odelia reached up to rub her palm against that manly scruff on his cheek. "I think we have been patient with you too long, dear boy." He tilted his head in question, and she dropped her hand, squaring her shoulders. "Tomorrow is Wednesday. I will expect you to attend the midweek prayer service tomorrow evening with us."

Phillip began shaking his head. "Aunt Odelia, I'm not ten years old, you know."

She raised a hand, palm out. "Spare me. Or humor me. Whatever it takes." She lifted her chin, saying, "You will recall the date, please."

He frowned, then a light dawned in his eyes. "Your wedding anniversary."

"And therefore, you will gift me with your regular attendance, henceforth, at prayer meeting."

Sighing, Phillip nodded. Then he leaned forward and pressed a kiss to the center of her forehead. She barely managed not to wrinkle her nose. Perhaps the manly scruff was not so thrilling as she'd imagined, and perhaps any romance between Carissa and her nephew was wishful thinking. It hardly mattered. The most important thing was that her nephew's eyes be opened to an important truth.

Perhaps his Heavenly Father would hear from him this very night. And maybe, just maybe, it would be the beginning of an ongoing conversation that would direct the rest of Phillip's life.

## *Chapter Seven*

Sliding the tray of dirty dinner dishes onto the dumbwaiter floor, Carissa marveled again at the old-fashioned but highly useful convenience. The little elevator certainly made life easier in a house this size. She wondered why more homes didn't use them. Then again, how many residences of this size even existed?

After sending the tray and its contents down to the butler's pantry, she intended to quietly gather the children and slip downstairs with them to wash the dishes. As much as she wanted to avoid running into Phillip, she refused to leave the mess for Hilda. It was bad enough that Hilda now cooked for them, along with the rest of the household. She wouldn't make additional work for her aunt by leaving the cleaning for her, too.

She sent the dirty dishes on their way and

turned back toward the suite, only to find Phillip standing behind her.

"I need to talk to you," he said.

She'd stayed inside all day just to avoid this very encounter. And to work, of course. Work was the excuse she'd given for not going downstairs for meals and for not joining Dallas and the children in the pool earlier this evening. It was perfectly legitimate. She'd made dozens of calls; she'd even reached her sales quota for the day—and avoided this very encounter. Until now.

"It won't take long," he promised, adding, "I have to leave for prayer meeting soon."

Carissa nodded, trying not to notice how nice he looked cleanly shaved and dressed in slim, dark slacks and a loose, pale olive shirt. Folding her arms, she leaned a shoulder against the paneled wall and noticed that he wore his loafers without socks. For some reason, that made her smile.

"I'm sorry about that kiss," he said softly, moving closer.

Just what every woman wanted to hear from the guy she'd awakened to find kissing her.

"I shouldn't have done it," he went on in a husky voice, "but you were so irresistible, all sleepy and sweet and mussed." He backed up a step, clearing his throat.

Carissa chanced a glance upward, her heart

in her throat. Irresistible? Her? Not on her best day had anyone described her as irresistible, let alone after a long hot day of hard manual labor. Any irritation she'd felt melted away like water droplets on a hot griddle. She tried to find something compelling to say and came up with "Oh."

He took her hand in both of his and said, "I don't want there to be any misunderstanding between us. I like you. I like you a lot." Her spirits literally soared—until he said, "But…"

Yeah, there was always a "but."

She snatched her hand free of his as he explained, "I'm not the right man for a woman like you."

"A woman like *me?*" she said. "A woman with kids, you mean."

"I can't even provide for myself," he went on. "How can I take care of a family?"

It was what she'd expected, of course, but the words hit her a reeling blow, nonetheless.

"Who asked you to?" she snapped.

"I know, I know," he said soothingly, "but there's no in-between with a woman like you. There's either friendship or marriage."

"That's right," she told him, lifting her chin.

She barely heard him as he prated on about her finer qualities. Individual words snagged briefly in her mind then floated away: *admiration, gumption, attraction…*. She heard the sound of his voice as he denigrated himself. He was irresponsible, selfish, immature. It was all nonsense, so she paid it no heed. Perhaps he wasn't conventional or predictable, but he'd taken responsibility for the needs of her and her children, at least in the short term, with no thought to his own personal comfort. As for immaturity, one man's maturity was another's tedium. No, what he really meant was that he didn't, *couldn't,* love her. Perhaps because she had too many children. Perhaps because she just wasn't enough for him to get past that.

Gradually, she became aware of an ache in the center of her chest. Shifting, she put her back to the wall and balled her hand into a fist, pressing it against that ache. Finally, she heard him say, "So, friends, then?"

Relieved that he had come to the end of what had been a painful monologue, she nodded dully and managed to reply, "Sure."

He blew out a breath. "Good. I'm glad."

"You're ready to go. Excellent."

Both Carissa and Phillip turned their attention in the direction of the Chatam sister who had arrived on the scene. Odelia stood near the end of the landing at the head of the stairs, her arm linked with that of her husband. She wore an ivory dress and a large fabric flower in her fluffy white hair. A corsage of roses and camellias had been pinned to her shoulder.

"We'd love for you to join us, Carissa," Odelia said. She patted Kent's arm lovingly. "It's our first wedding anniversary, and we'll be hosting a little celebration after prayer meeting."

Grinning, Kent touched the tip of his nose to hers, and she giggled, making the ropes of diamonds dangling from her earlobes swing.

"I—I didn't know," Carissa apologized. "Um, congratulations."

"Thank you, but you couldn't have known. You're all welcome to join us."

"I'm so sorry, but no. I've already bathed the children and gotten them ready for bed. We're just going to clean up our dinner dishes and turn in."

"Oh, what a pity," Odelia said, tilting her head. "Well, Chester said you wouldn't much be in the mood for a party yet. He and Hilda are going to pass on the party and just stop in for cake. I know! We'll see to it that Hilda saves you all some cake."

"That's very kind," Carissa began, thinking that the children would be bouncing off the walls if they consumed any extra sugar. "I try to limit the children's sweets."

"So they'll really love it," Phillip assured his aunt indulgently.

Carissa shot him a look, but he merely lifted an eyebrow. Odelia turned then for the stairs, directing her husband and nephew to follow. "Come along. Don't want to be late."

Phillip gave Carissa a helpless shrug as he obediently trailed his aunt and uncle.

"We'll pray for you, dear!" Odelia called as they disappeared down the stairs.

Carissa let her head fall back against the wall. She needed all the prayer she could get, if only because she was jealous of an elderly couple celebrating their first wedding anniversary.

The restaurant in the refurbished hotel in downtown Buffalo Creek provided a sumptuous setting for the anniversary celebration. Phillip toasted his giggling auntie and her beaming husband with a glass of soda and ate anniversary cake baked by Hilda but served by the restaurant staff. Quite a few people did the same, mostly family but also several friends. Phillip surprised himself by feeling like a fifth wheel. Everyone but him seemed to be paired up. Even Dallas arrived with a date, the same guy whom she'd sat next to during prayer meeting, Evan something, who looked as if he'd never done anything more strenuous than tie his shoelaces. Phillip discounted him as a serious presence in his sister's life the moment he met the man, but that didn't make him feel any less alone.

For the first time, he didn't quite know how to go forward on his own. Tonight at prayer meeting, he had found himself silently asking God to direct him. Spying his brother across the room, he wandered in that direction and minutes later had arranged to visit Asher in his law offices again next morning.

"Anything specific on your mind this time?" Asher asked.

Thinking about his conversation with Carissa earlier, Phillip made himself say, "Well, I'm ready to talk about that job now." So he wasn't what she needed right now. But that didn't mean that he couldn't ever be what she needed, not if he worked at it, did it?

Asher didn't exactly smile, but his face lightened. "Okay. I'll see what I can do."

Phillip wandered around the reception for a while longer, until he could hug Odelia and Kent, wish them happiness again and take his leave. He felt ridiculously lonely and as antsy as a beetle on a hot plate. He'd have gone for a long run in Seattle, but it was too hot for that here. He decided to swim laps in the pool at Chatam House, but after he climbed the stairs there, he couldn't make himself walk past Carissa's door.

He saw light coming from under the door, so

he took a chance and tapped. She answered the door in her bare feet, wearing baggy shorts and an oversize T-shirt. She'd caught her hair in a loose ponytail just below her left ear, and he wondered why she never seemed to let it down.

"I thought you'd be asleep by now," he said, keeping his voice low.

"I've been working," she said, leaning a shoulder against the doorjamb.

He frowned. "You're making calls at this time of night?" It was nearly ten o'clock.

"No, no. It's a side job."

He shook his head, then his curiosity got the better of him. "What sort of side job?"

She waved him into the room and padded over to the sofa. Sinking down onto the cushions, she lifted a notebook computer onto her lap. He sat down beside her and leaned in to look over her shoulder. The computer screen was gray with white and black characters. None of it made the least bit of sense.

"It's just gobbledygook."

"That gobbledygook translates into…" She made a series of keystrokes, and the screen transformed. "This." A sleek website popped up, complete with interactive graphics and pages of information, products and instructional videos. "We're adding widgets, phone apps and such."

"You can do that?"

"When I can get the work, I can do it."

He reached around her and scrolled through the site. "This is way cool."

"This is what I do," she said dismissively, closing the laptop and setting it aside.

She put her head back and craned her neck, relieving strain on her muscles, then covered a yawn with the back of one hand. "Sorry. Long day."

Phillip desperately wanted to put up his feet, loop his arm about her and snuggle, but he got the message. Their fledgling friendship wouldn't support that right now. She wanted him to go.

Reluctantly, he got to his feet, smiled and headed to the door, saying, "I won't keep you."

He was halfway across the room when she asked, "How was the party?"

Stopping, he turned back to answer. "Festive. Very festive."

She clasped her hands atop her knees. Very shapely knees. "Good."

He really should go. Instead, he said, "Prayer meeting was good." Oddly, he meant it.

"That's…that's nice."

Suddenly, he needed to tell her what he was thinking, needed to know what she thought. He took a step forward. "I didn't want to go. I just did it to please my aunt. I'm not even sure… That is, do you think God hears our prayers?"

Carissa seemed surprised. "Well, yes. Yes, of course."

"What I mean is, do you think He *wants* to hear our petty personal problems, our everyday, normal…junk?"

She obviously had to think about it. "I—I do. Yes."

"So, then, you think He answers those prayers, too?"

She nodded, then she bit her lip. "I used to. I mean, I do, but I guess I started doubting. I think I started to wonder if maybe He wasn't really listening anymore."

"I know what you mean," Phillip said, lifting a hand to the back of his neck. "When I was a boy, I didn't doubt that God heard or answered my silly little prayers, but as I got older, I started to wonder why He would bother."

"Why do we stop believing that He hears us?" Carissa asked. "Is it because we get beat up by life and think He's abandoned us?"

"Or do we just get so busy that we kind of forget," Phillip proposed, "and we start to think that we're small and unimportant and that we don't count?"

"I don't know," she said, "but before long it's

like that cousin we lost touch with or the sister we haven't heard from in years."

"I know what you mean," Phillip told her. "You start to think, 'Oh, they don't want to hear from me anymore.' But they do, don't they?"

"I think so," Carissa said. "At least, I think God wants to hear from us."

"Me, too," Phillip said. He hadn't thought so before, but he did now. Tonight, there in that room full of praying people, he had felt a part of something larger than himself and yet distinctly individual, as if God had singled him out.

"Sometimes I do wonder, though," Carissa admitted.

Phillip shook his head, suddenly quite sure, about her, at least. "No. Don't. God does want to hear our prayers. He wants to hear your prayers. I know He does."

"How can you be sure?"

"Because you are important," he told her. "You are important, Carissa. You're one of the most important people I've ever known. And if you ever doubt that, you just go look at those three kids in there." He jerked his head at the doorway to the bedroom hall, as certain as he'd ever been about anything in his life.

She stared at that doorway and smiled. Phillip walked out of the suite and went to his room, aware as never before of all that was missing in his own life. And why was that? Because he'd never had the time for such things before? Because he'd been too selfish and too wrapped up in his grand adventures to think of anything real and permanent?

Or because he simply hadn't met Carissa Hopper yet?

Asher phoned before seven the next morning to say that he'd set up a job interview for Phillip. Obviously, he'd called in a favor, probably the night before. Phillip obediently put on his best—okay, only—suit, said a stilted prayer and went to meet with the CEO of Sellers Financial Services.

Chuck Sellers was a nice fellow, about Asher's age and type. A businessman and professional through and through, in his mid to late forties, he looked fit and well-groomed, young despite the graying hair, the sort who had graduated college with a ten-year plan and stuck to it. In other words, he was Phillip's opposite in almost every way.

He glanced over Phillip's résumé, and they chatted for several minutes about mountain climbing, fishing and such things. After a while, Chuck suggested that he might have some "contract work" for Phillip in the future. They shook hands and parted, each fully aware that they had adequately taken the other's measure. Phillip was not cut out for a job with Sellers Financial Services, but because he had the necessary skills and was Asher's brother, Chuck would throw him whatever work he could when he could, just not now.

Phillip's relief was palpable. As much as he acknowledged the need for a job, he thanked God that this particular situation had not panned out. Wandering over to his brother's law office to inform him how the meeting had gone, he found Asher and his assistant fooling around with a smartphone app that they had purchased to facilitate the recording of depositions.

"You have no idea what a leap forward in technology this is," Asher declared, sitting back to film himself.

"You know what would be really sweet?" said the young man currently clerking for Asher. "An app that would telecast live transmissions of court proceedings into classrooms. Think about it. You could sell subscriptions based on field of study, torts, criminal law and so on."

"Think about the obstacles and permissions," Asher replied doubtfully.

"There would be some courts where it would be okay. Enough, I bet. Besides," argued the clerk, "these so-called reality apps are where it's at these days, just like reality TV. Of course, the episodes could always be archived, too. You could build a whole reference library."

Asher considered. "It could work." He shook his head. "But we don't know anything about technology."

"Or anyone who knows anything about technology," his assistant opined.

"I do," Phillip heard himself say.

Both gazes turned his way. "Someone in Seattle?" Asher asked, shifting in his seat.

"Uh, no," Phillip muttered. "She's here."

"Really?" Asher smiled, the light of speculation in his eyes. "Maybe you could ask *her* what she thinks about our idea."

"Maybe," Phillip murmured, his mind whirring with another possibility.

He recalled watching a video of a friend's climb on his own phone a few months ago and thinking how exciting it would have been if it had been live. He wondered if such a thing was possible. Carissa would know. It occurred to him that a live feed might have made it possible for help to reach his coworkers' party in time to save at least one or two of the climbers in that fall, and the realization shook him. Maybe it wouldn't have helped, but it could save someone in the future.

"Let me ask you a question," he said to his

brother. One question turned to ten as they probed the legalities of Phillip's proposal.

Phillip felt an excitement growing in him that he hadn't felt in a very long time, but he banked it. For one thing, he couldn't be sure of the viability of the idea. For another, something like this required careful planning and study. He saw no point in getting his hopes up until he'd done some solid research and crunched some numbers.

Talk turned, as it often did with Asher these days, to Phillip's niece, Marie Ella. "Why don't you come over tonight and see her?" Asher suggested.

Phillip balked, as he had every other time he'd been invited to get to know his new niece. Children who could walk and talk were one thing; infants were something else entirely. Shamelessly, he pulled out the only excuse he could find.

"Actually, my grief support group meets tonight."

Now that he thought about it, he really should attend tonight's meeting if only so he could urge Carissa to do the same. With her father's recent passing, how could she refuse to go? As predicted, Asher didn't argue.

"Well, I'm glad to see that my little brother isn't above getting some help when he needs it."

Phillip just shrugged.

"Let's say Saturday night, then, shall we?" Asher went on. "I'll invite Dallas and Petra. We'll make it a real family gathering."

What could Phillip do but chuckle and nod?

"Saturday it is," Asher reiterated happily.

Sighing inwardly, Phillip consoled himself with the thought that he'd have tonight with Carissa.

It was ten against one. Carissa knew it even before Phillip spoke. He had chosen his moment and laid his plan well. She'd come downstairs to fetch the children out of the pool so they could wash off the chlorine before dinner. Hilda and Chester served cold drinks to Hypatia and Magnolia on the expansive redbrick patio behind the great house, while Kent and Odelia paddled around in the big rectangular pool. As soon as Carissa called to the children, Phillip showed up with his sister.

"Dallas can do that," Phillip said, forestalling Carissa as she picked up the towels that the children had dropped at the edge of the patio. "I want to talk to you about tonight." His tone sounded conversational, but his voice was loud enough that everyone could hear.

"What about tonight?" she asked, knowing full well what he was going to say.

"It's Thursday," he pointed out, "grief support meeting night."

She immediately demurred. “Oh, the children need me here.”

“No, no, I’ll stay with them,” Dallas put in brightly.

“You should go, sugar,” Chester instantly urged, while Hilda nodded.

“Oh, do go, dear,” Hypatia implored, her sisters echoing her.

Even the children began to chant, bouncing up and down in the water at the edge of the pool. “Go! Go! Go!” Apparently, they believed that if she went with Phillip, they could continue to swim.

Carissa stood, the entire household against her, and frowned at her children. Then, resigned to her fate, she bent and picked up the towels, shaking them out one by one. It wasn’t as if she’d be alone with Phillip, after all. They were going to a meeting. The children began reluctantly wading from the pool. Dallas caught the towels and carried them to the kids, talking brightly about the evening she had planned for them.

Carissa looked over to Hypatia, who sat swathed in a thick terry-cloth robe, her feet encased in pristine canvas slippers. A wide-brimmed straw hat perched atop her head, and large, dark sunshades shielded her face. Magnolia, on the other hand, had prepared for an afternoon poolside by simply trading her muck boots for a pair of sandals.

Neither Kent nor Odelia was so circumspect. He sported a bright Hawaiian print shirt and flip-flops with his dark, knee-length swim trunks, while she wore a fluttery multihued cover-up of organza petals over a bright pink tankini with skirt and surplice top. Her swim cap resembled a pink turban wrapped around an artichoke, which pretty much described her oversize earrings, necklace and bracelet, all of which she wore into the pool. Thankfully, she'd left the pink, kitten-heel, open-toed mules poolside, along with a fluffy green towel.

"Phillip," Odelia called, "maybe you'd like a swim before dinner."

Carissa looked at his suit, rumpled now from a full day of wear, and the heavy shadow of his beard. Why did he have to be so very attractive?

"Maybe I will," he said with a blindingly white smile, which he then turned on Carissa. "What about you? Got time for a dip? Dallas will take care of the kids."

Suddenly, Carissa wanted nothing so much as to dive headlong into that cool, aqua-blue water with him, which was exactly why she dared not do it.

"No way," she said. "Even with your sister's help, it'll take some doing to get all three of the kids showered and dressed in time for dinner."

"Perhaps you'll join us in the dining room this evening," Hypatia invited, but Carissa put her off.

"Oh, I intend to put the kids straight into their pajamas," Carissa told her. "We'd best eat in our rooms again. But thank you. Another time."

"All right, then."

Dallas herded the children toward the house, Grace holding her hand and chattering happily. Carissa started after them, only to find herself stopped by Phillip's hand on her wrist.

"Be ready about a quarter of seven." She noted that he didn't ask; rather, he *told* her. Short of making a scene, she saw no option other than to swallow her indignation and go along with him. She gave him a curt nod and pulled away, hurrying after her children.

Behind her, she heard Hilda say quietly that the meeting would be good for her after Marshall's death. Tears sprang to Carissa's eyes, equal parts grief, frustration, anger and gratitude because she knew that these people had her best interests at heart. It wasn't their fault that she'd developed an unhealthy fascination for the wrong man.

Suddenly, she missed her dad so badly that she ached. If only he were still here, then she wouldn't be in this situation, living in the same house as Phillip Chatam. Then maybe she could keep her heart whole.

## *Chapter Eight*

The ache stayed with her as she shepherded the children through showers and got them into pajamas. Dallas helped, primarily with Grace, who treated Phillip's sister like her new best friend, which turned out not to be too far from the truth, as Carissa discovered when Dallas left to eat dinner with her family downstairs.

"'Bye, bffn!" Grace called after her.

Laughing, Dallas waved and blew her a kiss on her way out the door.

"What is this bffn?" Carissa demanded, parking her hands at her waist.

Grace just shrugged, smiling enigmatically, but Tucker supplied the answer. "Best friend for now."

Carissa spread her hands in confusion. "What does that mean, best friend *for now?*"

"It's just till you and Phillip—"

Nathan abruptly launched himself at his brother, fists flying. "You take that back!"

The boys rolled across the floor, pummeling each other. Grace instantly burst into noisy tears. By the time Carissa separated the boys and sent off everyone to bed in sulky shame, the bell was ringing to let her know that a delivery waited in the dumbwaiter. Thoroughly exasperated, Carissa stomped off to fetch the heavy tray. She laid out the meal, trying to make sense of what had just happened. She suspected that Phillip was somehow to blame, but when she tried to question the children over dinner, they all clammed up. Dallas came back up later, so Carissa applied to her for an explanation.

"I'm afraid it's all my fault," she said apologetically. "You know how kids are about that 'best friends forever' thing. I try to avoid that in my classroom with 'best friends for now' because, you know, things change. Kids move. Relationships shift."

"I see." That seemed reasonable.

Smiling, Carissa glanced at the clock on the mantel and saw that she had fewer than ten minutes to get dressed. Or she could just refuse to go to the meeting after all. Without really deciding either way, she headed for the bedroom and quickly threw on a simple sleeveless khaki dress that buttoned up the front, then she stepped into white sandals. She splashed water on her face, took down her hair and brushed it, dabbed on some lip gloss and shoved a white headband into place. That would have to do.

Hurrying back into the sitting room, she found Dallas stacking the dinner dishes on the tray. Carissa went to help her, but Phillip tapped on the door before they had finished. Wiping her hands on a linen napkin, Carissa directed the children to help Dallas with the cleanup then grabbed her handbag and hurried out.

"You look nice," he told her. He had shaved and put on jeans and a light blue button-up shirt. "I especially like your hair."

Her hand went immediately to the long, shaggy strands that hung down her back. She rarely wore her hair down because she hadn't had time or money to see a stylist in far too many months. It needed a good trim and shaping. But such things were luxuries that she could no longer afford. Still, he seemed sincere. She remembered, belatedly, to thank him.

His hand hovered around the small of her back as they descended the grand staircase. That made her nervous because this suddenly felt too much like a date. She didn't know why she'd come with him anymore. Was it because everyone expected it of her, for the grief support meeting or because, despite everything, she *wanted* this to be a date? She very much feared it was the latter.

She must be insane. He had told her, *warned* her that he wasn't in the market for a ready-made family. He'd stated bluntly that he wasn't the man for her. He had apologized for kissing her, and still she found herself attracted to him. For that reason alone, she had no business going anywhere with him. She started to pray silently. She'd been doing that more and more lately.

*Lord, don't let me make a fool of myself. I don't know what I'm doing anymore. I need You to guide me.*

They reached the foyer and crossed the floor. Phillip opened the door. He smiled down at her, and she walked through it, out onto the porch. The evening heat enveloped her. Phillip followed and shut the door closed behind them. Side by side, they walked down the steps and along the walkway to his vehicle. He helped her into the car and went around to get in behind the steering wheel.

They reached the church within minutes and were greeted warmly by the rest of the group. What shocked Carissa most, however, was how easily she found herself being drawn into the discussion.

"In one way, it was a relief," she said about her father's death. "He had suffered so much. In another, purely selfish way, I can't help missing him. The one person I always knew I could count on was my dad." Phillip's hand squeezed hers tightly. Funny, she hadn't even realized they were holding hands until that moment. She dabbed at her tears with a tissue that someone passed to her and smiled. "Dad wasn't very demonstrative. Hugs and kisses embarrassed him, but I knew how he felt."

"And he knew how you felt," Phillip assured her quietly.

After a while, talk turned to two women who had lost their husbands in the same auto accident. Their husbands hadn't known each other, but the women had become fast friends, united by their mutual loss.

"The funny thing is how much they had in common," one of them divulged.

"And how much we have in common," the other added.

"One of my friends who died was married," Phillip said. "His wife is a climber. She worked for the same company until she became pregnant with their first child. I used to joke that if I ever met anyone with whom I had so much in common as those two did, I'd marry her. Now all I think about is that she and their two kids were left alone. Mountain climbers are notoriously hard to insure, you know. I'm sure it's been tough for them."

People hastened to assure him that they would have Social Security to draw on, but Carissa felt stung. Had he contemplated marriage at some point? Was that what he wanted, a woman who could climb mountains with him? She couldn't imagine taking such chances when she had her children to consider.

After the meeting, as they were walking back to the car, she casually expressed her condolences for his loss. "I didn't realize that your friends had families."

Phillip nodded. "Everyone has a family. Just the one was married, though. No, that's not right. The client was married, too, and I understand he left his family very well provided for."

Carissa swallowed a lump in her throat and nodded. "That's good."

"I didn't really think about it until I met you, frankly."

"Yeah, well, it's been harder for me than I realized it was going to be," Carissa admitted. "Even after the first shock of it, you don't think it's going to change absolutely everything. But somehow it does."

"I'm sure it does. How can it not?"

"I don't know. You just think you're going to

keep things as normal as possible for your kids, only normal is never what it was, no matter what you do."

They got into the car and started back toward Chatam House. Thankfully, Phillip changed the subject.

"What do you think about a live-feed phone app?"

Surprised, she queried him on the subject, and they discussed the matter on the drive back. Phillip asked some pointed questions, which Carissa answered as best she could, telling him what she thought it would take to make something like what he seemed to have in mind work.

"So we'd need some hardware as well as the software," he realized. "Would that be terribly expensive?"

"Depends on your idea of expensive," she hedged. "I really couldn't estimate it without doing some research."

"Okay. So, are you too busy to do a little window-shopping tomorrow?"

She blinked at him. "You're serious about this?"

"I'm serious about looking into it."

She shrugged. "Well, I'm working tomorrow, so I won't be free until after five."

"Okay." He parked the car in front of the house

and killed the engine but made no move to get out. "Where do you think we should go? I don't usually shop for electronics."

She tried to think what was available locally then warned him against buying in person without checking online first. They got into the subject of computers and clones versus name brands. She had no idea of how long they sat there and talked until she suddenly yawned.

"I'm so sorry."

"No, I'm sorry," he said, opening his car door. "I've kept you up too late—you and Dallas both."

She checked her wristwatch and was stunned to see it was almost eleven.

"Oh, my!"

They hurried inside to find Dallas snoozing on the sofa in the master-suite sitting room. She sat up groggily when they came in, reported that the children had been perfect darlings, which Carissa doubted, waved off Carissa's effusive thanks and trudged out onto the landing. Phillip told Carissa good-night, promised to see her the next evening and followed his sister out. Carissa looked in on her sleeping children, turned off the lights and went to bed.

Her last thought was a repetition of her earlier prayer.

*Lord, please don't let me make a fool of myself over that man.*

She feared that was going to be more easily said than done, however.

# *Chapter Nine*

"Oh, come on," Phillip said, holding open the door of the Buffalo Creek café the next evening. "Even if Hilda held dinner back for us, she'll understand."

Carissa shook her head, but the smile he'd been seeing all evening flashed again. "I just hate to take advantage of your sister like this," she insisted, even as she slipped through the door. "This is the third time this week that she's babysat for me."

He chuckled. "I'll make it up to her, I promise, *after* I eat. Besides, I feel like celebrating. I never dreamed we could find what we need at such reasonable prices."

He felt happy, for no discernible reason. Yes, they'd found the hardware they'd been looking for, but Phillip had felt a quiet delight since he'd awakened that morning. Just knowing that he was going to spend time with Carissa had pleased him, and that pleasure had only grown throughout the evening.

"It pays to do your research," she reminded him as he steered her toward a booth.

"It pays to have an expert doing the research," he countered.

"I'm hardly an expert," she demurred, sliding onto the hard seat.

"That's not what the owner of the electronics shop said," Phillip reminded her. She deflected the compliment by looking around.

The picturesque diner, tucked into the back room of a dusty secondhand shop, featured lots of rusted, corrugated sheet metal, salvaged woods and cracked ceramics. A wholesome young waitress, costumed in overalls, her hair tied back with a bandanna, delivered menus printed on brown paper bags and water in pint jars, then trotted off to fetch iced tea while Phillip and Carissa perused their options.

Carissa chose a spinach, cheese and avocado sandwich with a side of fruit. Phillip unashamedly went for a gigantic chicken-fried steak, mashed potatoes, fried squash, cream gravy and biscuits. The food appeared quickly, too quickly to suit Phillip. They'd enjoyed a pleasant and productive time together. Carissa really knew her stuff, and Phillip naturally felt a certain excitement about the project, but what had him smiling, inside and out, couldn't be attributed to some possible phone app.

It was all wrong, of course. Carissa couldn't possibly be the woman for him. She needed a man who could support her and her children, someone like his brother, Asher, or his cousin Morgan, a college professor. Both were professional men with steady incomes. That type made good husbands and fathers. Didn't they?

On the other hand, not long ago his cousin Chandler hadn't been much more than a rodeo bum, and Garrett Willows, the aunties' former gardener, had been an ex-con before his pardon. They had both married and settled down happily. Everyone in the family had thought his cousin Reeves would remain a single father after his disastrous first marriage, but he'd married for a second time and seemed quite delighted with his new wife and family. Then there was his sister Petra and her carpenter husband, Dale. Phillip had expected Dallas to take a walk down the aisle one day but not ambitious, all-business Petra.

He just didn't know what to think anymore. He and Carissa had so little in common, but he felt something with her that he'd never felt with anyone else. He wasn't even sure that he liked it—even when it made him smile. She was just so prickly. He didn't think she even liked him, and maybe that was for the best. He decided to concentrate on the app for now and put the rest aside.

They finished their meal then chatted about the app and what they might do with it. He realized that he'd need to make some phone calls before they went any further. If none of the mountain-climbing guides were interested in wearing the tiny cameras that he and Carissa had found, then what would be the point in designing the application that would allow subscribers to follow the climb live?

Carissa insisted on returning to the house to be sure that the children had gotten to bed at a decent hour, even though Dallas would have made sure they had. They turned onto the drive in front of the mansion at ten minutes of nine. As the car crested the rise, however, Carissa sat up straight and let out a strangled sound. A late-model domestic luxury auto sat parked in front of the walk.

"Looks like the aunties have company," Phillip murmured, confused by her reaction.

"Not the aunties," she said enigmatically. She bailed out of the car before he could ask her what she meant, not even bothering to close the door behind her.

Phillip hastily parked, hurried around to close

the car door and followed. He found her in the front parlor with his aunts, Kent, Chester and a tanned, fit, blond couple, who looked as if they belonged in Hollywood rather than Texas.

Seated on the antique settee, the woman crossed her long, slender legs, displaying stiletto heels and a skirt both too short and too tight. She tossed a length of thick, golden hair from her slender shoulder with a bejeweled hand sporting long white-tipped fingernails and batted her false eyelashes at Phillip before smiling up at Carissa with frosty pink lips.

"Hello, sweetheart," she purred.

Carissa audibly ground her teeth together before spitting out two words that shocked Phillip to his toes.

"Hello, Mother."

*Mother?* Phillip had to work to keep his jaw from dropping to the floor. A second, closer look showed him the fine lines that no amount of cosmetics could hide or plastic surgery could erase.

"I'd have come sooner, darling, but I know how busy you are, and then, of course, there was the little matter of *locating* you."

"My cell phone number hasn't changed," Carissa pointed out drily.

Carissa's mother pursed her too-pouty lips. "What good would a phone call have done? You need more help than that, surely."

Hypatia cleared her throat, looked to Carissa and gently said, "Your mother seems to be of the opinion that she should be allowed to take your two youngest children away with her."

Carissa threw up her hands. "Oh, it's Grace *and* Tucker you want now?"

False eyelashes batted over eyes of such bright blue that they had to be the product of colored contacts. "We only want to help."

"By taking my children? You've been offering to *help* by taking Grace since Tom died. Why is Tucker suddenly part of the plan?"

"Why not Nathan?" Phillip wanted to know, insulted on the boy's behalf. Okay, so the kid could be a tad difficult, but he'd lost his dad, his home, his grandfather. He was bound to be touchy. That didn't make him a problem child.

Carissa's mother turned to Phillip, purring, "And you are?"

Realizing belatedly that it wasn't his place to speak, Phillip shifted from one foot to the other. "Phillip Chatam."

"Alexandra Hedgespeth." She introduced herself with an ingratiating smile. Waving a hand at the strange man standing behind her, she said, "My husband, Leander."

Nodding, Leander Hedgespeth leaned forward and stretched out a beefy hand. He looked to be decades younger than Alexandra, though if he kept frequenting tanning salons, no doubt it would soon be difficult to tell.

Blinded by Leander's professionally whitened smile, Phillip shook hands with the man then stepped back as Carissa baldly stated, "She doesn't want Nathan. Or Tucker. She wants Grace. She always has."

The truth of that was written all over Alexandra's heavily made-up face. She wanted Grace with the same lust that she wanted youth and beauty. Phillip saw it but didn't understand it.

"I love my granddaughter," Alexandra proclaimed grandly. "She's very special. But that doesn't mean I don't love my grandsons, too."

"Oh, please." Carissa frowned and folded her arms.

"You know she'd be happier with me," Alexandra argued. "They all would be." She smoothed her hair with one long-nailed hand, adding, "I just don't have room for all three of them right now."

"And since Grace wouldn't willingly go with you on her own," Carissa pointed out, "you thought you'd take Tucker along to entice her."

"You can't support them, Carissa," Alexandra accused. "Look at you! Reduced to taking charity from strangers."

"She has family here," Chester pointed out

testily. "Where were you when the bank took the house in Dallas?"

"I've already told you that I don't have room for more than two guests," Alexandra snapped.

"Oh, and I suppose my brother did?" Chester shot back.

"Well, if you're willing to live like dogs in a kennel…"

"Dad was willing to do anything it took," Carissa said in a voice trembling with anger.

"Anything but live like he had an ounce of pride," Alexandra grumbled. Odelia gasped, and Alexandra immediately backtracked, saying, "Oh, let's don't argue. I only want to help."

"You're not taking my children," Carissa stated firmly, "so get that idea out of your head now."

"But you obviously can't take care of them yourself."

"Oh, yes, she can," Phillip refuted, stepping up behind Carissa. "She's had some tough breaks, but Carissa is a computer expert, and she's an excellent mother. She's done just fine by her kids—better than most could have under the same circumstances."

"I have to agree," Hypatia said. "Frankly, we expected some upset within the household when Carissa and the children moved in, but we've hardly noticed their presence." She then turned a look on Carissa, adding, "We would actually welcome a bit more interaction."

Carissa bowed her head. "Thank you, ma'am. I'll bear that in mind."

Hypatia shot a loaded look at Phillip and said, "I expect you to remind her."

He opened his mouth then shut it again, settling for a noncommittal nod.

"Well, you can't stay here indefinitely," Alexandra pointed out.

"I should think that would be for us to decide," Odelia said with great dignity.

"I'll only be here until I save enough to get into a place of our own," Carissa declared. "That was always the intent."

"You'd have had an easier time of it if you'd have let me take Grace before," Alexandra declared.

"Never," Carissa vowed. "Grace is my daughter, and she's going to be raised by me. Period."

Alexandra made an exasperated sound. "Well, let me see her at least. Them, I mean. I came all this way—can't I at least see my grandchildren?"

Carissa rolled her eyes. "Mother, do you have any idea what time your grandchildren, most children in fact, go to bed?"

Alexandra rolled her shoulders and lifted her chin. "I only want to *see* them. I'm not going to wake them."

Phillip cleared his throat, leaned in close and murmured to Carissa, quite audibly, "Perhaps she could go upstairs and just look in on them *as she's leaving.*"

Carissa frowned but gave in. "Oh, all right. Come on."

Alexandra shot Phillip a pleased, conspiratorial smile as she rose sleekly to her high-heeled feet. She slunk off after Carissa, who paused only to slide Phillip a frowning glance that seemed to ask if he was coming. Surprised, he didn't immediately follow—until he realized all three of the aunties were staring at him in silent rebuke. Bowing apologetically, he set out after Carissa and her mother. Behind him, he heard Odelia offer Leander Hedgespeth a cup of tea.

"Ah, no, thank you," he said heartily, "but I wouldn't turn down something stronger."

At that, Phillip had to pause and look back. His aunties exchanged expressions of confusion before Odelia offered, "A soft drink, perhaps?"

It was Hedgespeth's turn for puzzlement. "Uh, actually, I was hoping..." Leander's perfectly groomed brows rose in tandem the moment he realized that no alcohol would be available. Phillip choked back a chortle and sprinted off after Carissa and her mother. He caught them at the bend in the stairs. Alexandra was quietly haranguing Carissa about Grace.

"You know I can give her everything she wants."

"Children shouldn't have everything they want."

"You know what I mean."

"What I don't know is why you want her. It's not like you wanted me or even Lyla."

"That's not true."

"Couldn't prove it by me."

"Besides, it's not for me."

"Well, it's certainly not for her because you know that Grace doesn't want to live with you."

"She would if you'd stop tearing me down to her."

Carissa rolled her eyes. "You'd be amazed how rarely we discuss you, Mother."

"What about your husband?" Phillip heard himself ask. "How does he feel about raising a child?"

Alexandra stopped dead in her tracks right at the top of the stairs and swallowed, straining her too-taut throat, before she broke into a wide smile, her false eyelashes batting rapidly. "Leander would like to be a father, now that you mention it, and he would be a good one, too. No concerns there."

She stepped onto the landing and swept past

Carissa, who hung back long enough to look at Phillip and mutter, "Finally, I get what's going on here."

Phillip could only shake his head. Obviously, all Alexandra Hedgespeth cared about was keeping her much younger husband happy. It was doubtful the couple could easily adopt, given the difference in their ages. Well, he would never allow that woman or anyone else to take Carissa's child from her. Never. He didn't question or examine that determination. It simply *was.* Clapping a supportive hand on Carissa's shoulder, he followed her onto the landing and then along the left side of the landing to the master suite in the corner.

As soon as they came through the door into the sitting room, Dallas rose from the sofa, greeted everyone with a nod, shook hands with Alexandra, whom Carissa introduced as her mother, and watched in some confusion as Carissa led Alexandra through the back hallway and into the children's rooms. Phillip whispered that he'd explain later, then he followed Carissa and her mother, while Dallas left the suite.

They went first to the boys' room. Phillip saw that Nathan had constructed a barrier of pillows between his side of the bed and Tucker's, for good reason, apparently. Tucker sprawled over his half of the bed, an arm flung over the pillows so that one hand rested against Nathan's forehead. One of Tucker's legs dangled off the bed. Phillip made a mental note to see that the boys' bunk beds were moved into the room.

Nathan shifted from beneath his brother's hand and opened his eyes. He smiled wanly at his mom, frowned at Phillip, then his face froze like ice as his grandmother trilled her fingers in a little wave. He abruptly rolled over, giving her his back. Alexandra folded her arms irritably. Phillip resisted the urge to pat the boy in approval.

Carissa went around the bed adjusting Tucker's limbs, straightening the covers and whispering in Nathan's ear before leading the way out of the room. Alexandra followed and, as usual, Phillip turned to bring up the rear. To his shock, Nathan suddenly shot upright in the bed, reached across his sleeping brother and snagged Phillip by the back pocket of his pants. Too stunned to do anything more than look down in surprise, Phillip stared openmouthed.

"Don't let her take Grace," Nathan pleaded in a whisper. "Please. Hide her if you got to."

Phillip blinked and let a hand fall on the boy's thin shoulder. "Don't worry. Grace isn't going anywhere. Your mother would never allow it."

"She might not be able to stop it. We got no money."

"She's not by herself," Phillip assured the boy.

"She has all of us Chatams behind her now. Your family will not be broken up. I promise."

Nathan looked vastly relieved, but as he sank back onto his pillow, his arms folding behind his head, some of his old contrariness reasserted itself. "You don't really got anything to say about it, though, do you?"

"Then why did you ask me for my help?" Phillip countered quietly, turning away. He glanced at Tucker, amazed to find the boy still sleeping peacefully. Even in sleep, he looked like the charming little scamp that he was. "Don't worry," he said to Nathan before slipping from the room.

By the time Phillip made his way to Grace's room, Alexandra was sitting on the side of the bed with the girl in her lap. Either she had not been asleep, either, or had awakened easily. Carissa seemed none too happy about the situation, but Grace appeared pleased enough to see her grandmother, whom she called Lexi.

Alexandra made a great fuss, hugging Grace and petting her hair. She talked about buying pretty dresses and dolls. Once she asked, "Would you like that, sweetheart?"

Grace smiled and nodded enthusiastically, but Phillip had the feeling that Grace was indulging her grandmother rather than the other way around.

After a few minutes, Carissa walked forward and held out her arms, saying, "It's time you were asleep, young lady."

Grace went immediately and without argument to her mom, smiled down at her grandmother and chirped, "Good night, Lexi."

Alexandra rose, dabbed at her eyes and burbled, "Good night, my darling."

She hurried from the room as Carissa tucked Grace into bed. Phillip stayed long enough to drop a kiss onto Grace's forehead before following them both into the sitting room. Alexandra stood with her hands over her face as if hiding tears, but Phillip noticed that when she dropped them, her makeup still looked perfect and her eyes were dry. She smoothed the hem of her knit top and swayed over to Phillip, doing her best to appear sad.

"I'm sorry that the Chatams have been dragged into all this," she said. "I'd have prevented it if I could have."

Phillip drew his brows together. "The Chatams haven't been dragged into anything. My aunts are always eager to help when they can."

"Oh, I'm sure that's true," Alexandra hastened to say, "but it wasn't necessary in this case."

"No? You said yourself that you don't have room for Carissa and the children."

"Well, not all of them," Alexandra hedged,

"but we'd gladly do what we can. I mean, family should help family. Don't you agree?"

"Of course."

"And family should go to family first."

"Which is exactly what Carissa did," he pointed out, "by going to her father and then her uncle."

Alexandra ignored that, saying with some exasperation, "If she'd let me provide a home for Grace and Tucker, this whole thing would have been far easier."

"For whom?" Phillip had to ask. "Not for Carissa, and not for the children, either."

"Just because my daughter is stubborn and unforgiving," Alexandra began hotly, but Phillip was having none of that.

"You say 'stubborn.' I say 'determined,' and thank God for it, because from what I can tell, she's made it this far on sheer determination and not much else."

"You don't understand," Alexandra insisted, shaking her head. "She's never forgiven me for following my heart, no matter how many times I've tried to explain. My daughter is stubborn and unforgiving. And Nathan is just like her."

"I don't pretend to know what's between you and your daughter," Phillip stated firmly, feeling his temper spike, "but Nathan is a child, a little boy who has lost way too much already.

All Nathan is guilty of is doing his best to help his mom, who hasn't exactly had it easy the past several years."

Alexandra waved that away. "I've been dealing with Carissa and Nathan all that time. I've tried and tried with both of them. I really have, and it's gotten me nowhere. Neither of them cares whether I'm happy or not."

"Carissa is your daughter. Nathan is your grandson," Phillip lectured. "That entitles them to unconditional love from you. They are not here to feed your emotional needs. It's the other way around. That doesn't mean you have to support bad behavior from either one of them, but you don't get to sweep Grace and Tucker off to some fairy-tale life and relegate Nathan and Carissa to a life of misery without them. Carissa and her children are a family. You have no right to interfere with that."

"I have more right than you do!" Alexandra retorted.

"Maybe so," he conceded, "but Carissa's got me in her corner, just the same, and all the rest of the Chatams will line up right behind us. Mark my word. And for what it's worth, lady, in my opinion, Carissa and Nathan each are worth a hundred of you because at least they are honest about what they feel and why."

Alexandra squared her shoulders, let out a

huff, spun on her heels and marched out of the room, saying grandly, "I'll be back."

Growling, Phillip executed his own about-face and nearly bowled over Carissa, who stood there staring at him as though he'd grown a third eye. Embarrassed, Phillip cleared his throat. She swept past him and went to the sofa. Dropping down on the cushion, she put her head in her hands. Phillip followed warily. She suddenly looked up, sniffed and glanced away.

"Are you crying?"

Shrugging, she shook her head. "I never know whether to laugh or cry where my mother is concerned."

"Ah."

She scooted over a few inches. He took it as an invitation to sit down and lowered himself gingerly to the sofa beside her. Carissa clasped her hands together and stretched them out in front of her.

"My mother left my dad for another man," Carissa explained. "She needed 'excitement,' someone with 'style.' Apparently being faithful and hardworking rules out those things in her world."

"So she left him for Leander."

Carissa looked up in surprise. "Oh, my, no. Leander is husband number four, maybe number five or even six. There are long periods when we don't see or hear from her at all, so who knows?"

"I see."

"This thing with Grace really got serious after she married Leander, maybe three and a half years ago."

"I'd guess that he wants children and she can't give them to him," Phillip ventured.

"You may be right about that," Carissa mused. Sighing, she passed a hand across her forehead and confessed, "What scares me is that I might eventually have to let her take in my children because I won't be able to provide for them myself."

"That's not going to happen."

"If I can't make a home for them on my own, she might be able to make a court case," Carissa pointed out in an agonized whisper.

Phillip smiled supportively. "I doubt it, but if she should try, I'm sure that my brother, Asher, will represent you. He's an attorney, you know."

Carissa threw up her hands at that, scoffing. "How can I afford an attorney when I can't even afford an apartment?"

"Now, now." Phillip looped his arm around her, pulling her close to his side in an effort to calm and comfort her. "There's no sense in borrowing trouble. Has your mother said anything about bringing a court case?"

"No," Carissa admitted in a small voice, relaxing against him and laying her head on his shoulder.

Phillip smiled and resisted the urge to kiss the top of her head.

"Well, then. We won't worry about it. But we will be prepared in case she starts trouble. I'll speak to my brother about it. Okay?"

She hesitated for several long seconds, but then she nodded. "Okay."

He folded her a little tighter. "Everything's going to be fine. You'll see."

"You don't know that," Carissa argued, but he had the feeling that it was just for form's sake.

"Everything is going to be fine," he repeated, fighting to keep a chuckle from breaking into his tone. Alexandra was right about one thing. This woman was nothing if not stubborn. Right now, that didn't seem like such a bad thing to him.

Carissa said nothing for a long while, but then her hand drifted up to brush his chest, and she turned up her face, whispering, "Thank you."

He didn't realize that she meant to kiss him until she did it, her lips pressing lightly against his. His heart swelled, and without thinking, he angled his head, drawing her nearer—until he caught movement from the corner of his eye and froze. Instinctively, he lifted his head and looked in that direction.

Nathan peeped out of the hallway entrance.

Taking her cue from Phillip, Carissa straightened, turning her attention in the direction of the hallway, but Nathan had already jerked back out of sight.

Phillip wisely let his arms fall away and a moment later folded his hands over his knees.

"Well," he said lightly, "we've all had an emotionally trying evening. I'll let you get some rest."

"Yes, thank you." She sounded tired and...disappointed? Embarrassed, perhaps, but not disappointed, surely. Getting slowly to her feet, she added, "And thank you for what you said to my mother, too."

Ah. That explained the kiss, then. Gratitude, not attraction. If anyone was disappointed, it was him, but he tried not to let it show.

"No problem."

Shooting another glance at the empty hall doorway, he left her and went in search of his aunties. He'd meant what he'd said about Carissa having the Chatams behind her. Asher would most definitely help, and the aunts, too, but Phillip would leave nothing to chance. He wanted the entire weight of the Chatam influence behind Carissa and her children, whether she needed it or not. Just in case.

# *Chapter Ten*

Pirouetting in the center of the floor, Grace bumped into Tucker, who promptly circled her throat with his forearm.

"Now I got a hostage."

"No fair!" Nathan bawled. "Mountain lions don't take hostages."

Carissa covered the mouthpiece of the telephone headset with one hand and gestured sternly toward the bedroom with the other. She knew it was unfair to ask them to play only in their rooms, but she dared not work in the master bedroom and let them play here in the sitting room unsupervised. They'd already knocked over the lamp once. Thankfully, it hadn't broken. Besides, the bed did not make a comfortable workspace, especially when she was frustrated because she hadn't closed a sale all morning.

Tucker made a growling sound, showing his

displeasure, while Grace sighed then plopped down among her coloring books and dolls to begin gathering them. Nathan, as usual, started to argue.

"Aw, Mo-o-om. It's no fun in there."

Carissa held up a finger and made the keystrokes necessary to activate the microphone in her headset via her laptop. "That's right, sir. Twenty-four-hour-a-day access by telephone and online. If you're at your computer, you can go to our website now and see the levels of service available. I'll be happy to send the link and wait for you to connect." Glaring at Nathan, she typed in the email address and routed the link. While her client made the connection, she muted her end of the connection again and shook her finger at the children.

"I am sick and tired of telling you three to calm down."

"We want to go out," Nathan whined.

"I can't go outside now. I have to work."

"We can go out by ourselves. We won't get into trouble."

Before she could do more than roll her eyes at that, a knock sounded on the suite door, and Tucker scampered to answer it. Odelia and Phillip entered the room. Odelia wore a huge cardinal-red hat and a white dress with a pleated skirt and big red polka dots. White, feathered balls swung from her earlobes. Phillip wore his usual cargo shorts and T-shirt, along with a wide grin.

As the children watched, fascinated, Odelia tugged on a pair of white, lacy gloves, announcing grandly, "We've come to take the children to the park."

Tucker literally crowed at that news, while Grace leaped up and clapped, pirouetting in midair. Carissa could have cried with relief.

"Oh, thank you, but are you sure? It isn't too much trouble?"

"No, no. It's all planned," Phillip said with the wave of a hand. "A Saturday in the park will be fun for all of us. Hilda is packing a picnic basket, and Kent is bringing around the car. We'll have them home before the hottest part of the day."

"In time for a cool swim," Odelia put in.

Carissa closed her eyes in gratitude then held up a hand for quiet as her client came back on the line. "Yes, that's correct. Seven ninety-nine a month includes automatic backup and storage of everything that appears on your desktop." She nodded and went on. "You just fill out the online form. I'll send you a confirmation email with telephone numbers. I suggest you make a note of them. Click on the link to activate the account, and the icon will appear on your desktop. You can find the telephone numbers there, too, but if your computer is on the blink, you'll want those numbers handy elsewhere." After another moment she was able to say, "Thank you. We appreciate your business." Finally, a sale.

She ended the call and addressed Odelia. "I'm sorry, but that's the first sale I've made today. I couldn't put him on hold again."

"No need to apologize. You're working. We'll just get out of your way."

"Come on, kids," Phillip said, lifting an arm.

"Everyone have their shoes?" Carissa asked.

While Tucker and Grace hurried to find their discarded shoes, Nathan hopped out of reach, shouting, "I'm not going! I'm not going!" With that, he bolted for the bedroom.

Stunned, Carissa sat frozen.

Now what? Hadn't he just begged to go out?

She stared helplessly at Phillip, who said pointedly, "He saw us last night."

Carissa shook her head. "I don't understand. Saw us?"

Phillip gusted out a sigh and shot a glance at Odelia, muttering, "On the couch."

Carissa recalled the kiss, her cheeks heating. She quickly looked away, her hand going to her throat.

"That...that was my fault." She shoved aside the laptop and got to her feet, tearing off the headset and dropping it to the sofa cushion as she started forward. "I'll explain it to him. When he knows what his grandmother attempted—"

Phillip stopped her in midstride, his hands clasping her upper arms. "Are you sure that's wise?"

"You're right. Nathan already carries a heavy enough load as it is, and that's my fault, too. He's tried to replace his father with the younger children, and I've let him, even though I've known all along that it's too much responsibility for a boy his age."

"Let's not place blame," Phillip said, his voice wrapping around her like a warm blanket. "I'm sure you've done what you thought was best."

"Perhaps Phillip should speak to Nathan, dear," Odelia suggested gently.

"Me?" Phillip queried.

"Man-to-man, so to speak," Odelia said.

"Oh. Well, if you think that'll help."

Carissa hesitated, one hand going to the back of her neck. "Uh, I—I'm not sure that's… I mean, I doubt he'll be receptive."

Phillip shrugged. "Won't hurt to try."

Carissa sucked in a deep breath then let it out again. "Go ahead."

What was the worst that could happen? Nathan would dig in his heels and refuse to go to the park with his brother and sister. It would serve him right, and she could still get some work done. Maybe she'd have an opportunity to speak with her eldest son in private, too.

Folding her hands, she smiled lamely at Odelia Chatam Monroe and sent up a silent prayer.

Phillip gathered his courage as he marched toward the bedroom. He didn't knock on Nathan's door—why give the boy another chance to reject him?—just opened it and stepped inside.

Nathan didn't waste any time beating around the bush. Phillip had barely closed the door before the boy rolled into a sitting position on the side of the bed and demanded, "Are you going to marry my mom?"

The question took Phillip by surprise, but a moment's reflection lessened the shock of it. Of course Nathan would view every man who came into Carissa's life as a potential husband. Phillip himself had already known that, which meant that he should have been able to give Nathan the firm denial that he so obviously wanted.

What he actually said was "I doubt it." *That* was more stunning than the question itself.

Nathan glared and asked, "How come?"

Phillip searched for an answer. "For one thing, people who get married should be in love."

"And you're not in love with my mom?"

Oh, boy. He'd walked straight into that one. After gasping like a fish out of water for several seconds, he did the only thing he could: he answered honestly.

"I don't know."

"Why not? On account of us kids?"

"No. I'll admit that I've never thought of myself as husband or father material, but if I was going to be someone's father, I would be honored to be yours."

Nathan thought that over some then shook his head. "Grace and Tucker maybe, but not me. I know you don't like me."

"That's not true. I have a lot of respect for you, Nathan."

"Like I'd believe *you* about anything," Nathan sneered.

"I don't like the way you act sometimes," Phillip admitted. "But you stepped in to help your mom after your dad died, even though, after her, you're the one who misses him most. I'm not sure I'd have done that myself. I'm more like Tucker, frankly—all fun and games."

Nathan narrowed his eyes behind the lenses of his glasses then looked away. "Tucker's okay most of the time," he muttered.

Phillip hid a smile. If Tucker was okay, then he, Phillip, must be okay, too, in his way.

"Put your shoes on," he said. "Let's go to the park."

Making a great show of his reluctance, Nathan

slowly got off the bed, went to the closet and found a pair of shoes. He stomped his feet into them without untying the strings and dragged himself toward the door. As he stood next to Phillip, he looked up and asked, "My mom's pretty, isn't she?"

Phillip's breath caught. Did this kid actually *want* him to marry his mom?

"Your mom's beautiful," Phillip told him flatly. "But I'm not sure she really likes me very much."

Screwing up his face, Nathan gave his head the barest of shakes, as if to say that Phillip was too stupid to live. "She likes you."

Phillip tilted his head, studying Nathan like a bug. "What makes you think so?"

"She kissed you, didn't she?"

Phillip's heart skipped a beat, but he kept his expression blank. "She did, but maybe not for the reason you think."

Nathan rolled his eyes, yanked open the door and marched out, as if to his doom. Phillip stood there a moment longer, wondering if Nathan knew something he didn't or if wishful thinking was about to get him in way, way over his head.

By the time he entered the sitting room, Odelia and Carissa had herded the children to the door. Phillip joined them there, and they all quickly took their leave of Carissa. Phillip ignored her curious looks, uncertain himself what had really happened with Nathan. True to his nature, he simply put the matter out of mind.

Phillip was used to an active lifestyle, but in the space of the next few hours, the children wore out him and the other two adults supervising them. Phillip wound up chasing Nathan and Tucker all over the park while Odelia and Kent took turns pushing Grace on the swings and the merry-go-round. She obligingly matched her pace to theirs, making Phillip muse that Grace often seemed to be a happy adult in a child's body, while too many adults behaved like spoiled children. Nathan and Tucker, on the other hand, were active little boys. They went from driving on imaginary roads to fighting imaginary battles to riding imaginary dinosaurs, and all of it involved running, jumping, climbing, hiding and making loud noises. Phillip had his hands full making sure they didn't get lost or hurt. He was ready to tie them to the picnic-table bench by the time they all sat down to eat lunch.

Thankfully, Hilda had packed such a hearty meal, crammed with all their favorites, that the children stuffed themselves. Afterward they could barely keep their eyes open. Odelia spread a blanket in the shade of a tree, and even Nathan dozed for a few minutes, but then he and Tucker were up and off again. Odelia and Kent looked positively exhausted by the time they got the picnic basket repacked and the children loaded back into the car. Even Odelia's hat was drooping.

On the way home, Kent asked the children how they liked living at Chatam House. Tucker and Grace had only good things to say, but Nathan shrugged and grumbled, "It'd be okay if I had my own bed."

Phillip decided then to get those bunk beds moved into the master suite ASAP.

Hypatia and Magnolia agreed to watch the children swim in the pool while Phillip, Odelia and Kent went upstairs to clean up and, in Kent and Odelia's case, nap. Phillip was expected at his brother's for an early dinner, and he'd promised to pick up Dallas on the way. After delivering the children back to the suite in their wet bathing suits and towels, he asked Carissa for a report on her day and was pleased that she was pleased.

"I know you engineered this outing," she said, "and I thank you."

"Well, if it helps you work…"

"Yes," she said, "the more money I make, the sooner we'll be out on our own." That wasn't his point, but he let it stand. "This will all be so much easier once school starts again," she went on. "We'll be in our own place, and even Grace will be out of the house half days."

"That will be helpful," Phillip commented

idly, thinking how to broach the subject of the bunk beds. “Listen, I know you don’t want to get too comfortable here, but Nathan really wants his own bed. Would you mind if I set up the bunk beds?”

She seemed troubled by the prospect. “Oh, I’d hoped to avoid that.”

“I think it really would help.”

“It would give the boys more room to play,” she considered.

Phillip took that as consent and promised to take care of it then hurried off to pick up Dallas.

They arrived at Asher and Ellie’s sprawling, modern, blond-brick house just as their sister Petra and her husband, Dale, did. Dale was in the construction business with his father, and Petra had taken over the day-to-day operation of the office. Phillip still couldn’t get used to seeing his once-quite-sophisticated sister in jeans and casual tops, but he loved the fact that she always seemed to be smiling. Petra had a soft look about her now, a warmth, that he’d never suspected was part of her personality. Dale seemed his usual easygoing self, nodding as Phillip asked to borrow a truck again in order to move a set of bunk beds from storage to Chatam House.

“I’ll do you one better,” Dale said. “I’ll help you move them later tonight.”

Phillip grinned, and they shook hands on it. "Can't pass up that deal."

Asher let them in and led them to the living room, his two-month-old daughter cradled in the crook of one arm. She didn't stay there for long. First Dallas, then Petra snatched her up. When Ellie called from the kitchen, Petra passed the baby to Dale as casually as if she was passing him a puppy or a pillow, and Dale took her just as easily, cradling her tiny head in his palm and making a bed for her of his forearms. She kicked and cooed and generally seemed to be trying to join in the conversation as the men chatted about golf and baseball and Asher's passion, soccer. Then, suddenly, for no apparent reason, she screwed up her little face and screamed. Horrified, Phillip couldn't believe it when both Asher and Dale began to laugh.

"Guess we know what that means," Asher announced, rising from the sofa in the sunken living area. Before he could say or do anything else, Ellie swept in to throw the baby onto her shoulder.

"I'll take care of it."

She went out again, and only as she and the infant disappeared did Phillip realize that they had taken a rather loamy smell with them.

"That child cannot abide a dirty diaper," Asher

said with unusual pride. Phillip could only shake his head.

"Ought to be a snap to toilet train, then," Dale observed idly.

Phillip coughed into his hand and changed the subject. "We have a situation at Chatam House I need to discuss with you, Ash."

He gave his brother a quick rundown on Carissa's situation with her mother. As always, Asher listened attentively. Finally, he spoke.

"Well, there's nothing to be done unless this Alexandra acts. If she forcibly takes one or more of the children, or if she files suit, even if she should file a complaint with Child Protective Services, then Carissa can intervene legally. Otherwise..." He spread his hands.

Phillip nodded. "I understand. But if the need arises, you'll help Carissa protect her children, won't you? She's a wonderful mother, and she's done the very best she could under very tough circumstances. I want her to know she'll have help."

"She's Chester's niece and the aunties have taken her in," Asher replied. "That's enough for me."

"Great," Phillip said, relieved—not that he'd really doubted Asher would help—but then Ash grinned.

"With you championing her cause, though,

I'm wondering if legal representation is enough. Maybe we should be preparing to welcome her to the family."

Phillip's mouth fell open. "Why does everyone automatically assume—"

The words died as Ellie unceremoniously dropped his niece into his hands, declaring, "Sounds like you should be getting used to this. I have to get back to the kitchen and take care of dinner."

Phillip made a strangling sound and bobbled the child but managed not to drop her. She seemed not to mind, if her toothless grin was any indication. To his surprise, she stared straight into his eyes and lifted a brow as if to ask what he thought of her. Having never held a baby before, he was too busy trying not to break her to form many impressions at first, but soon he began to realize how soft and tiny she was. Soft, tiny and very real. This was a person, a whole, complete person in a tiny, gurgling, strangely adorable package.

He thought of Grace, and then he remembered a box of baby photos that he'd stumbled across—well, accidentally dumped—while helping Carissa clean out the apartment. Images flashed before his mind's eye: Carissa with very long hair, holding one of the boys on her lap and mugging for the camera, baby smiles and baby feet, fat tummies and chubby hands, a single tooth in a wide smile, drooping diapers and first steps.

He concentrated on the niece he'd avoided all these weeks, this little bit of helpless humanity in his lap. Soon she would be as engaging and charming as Grace. Or not. He couldn't really imagine any little girl being as engaging and charming as Grace, but Marie Ella would almost certainly be bright and athletic and treasured, and he would love her. He did love her, soft, sweet, little thing that she was. He swallowed a lump in his throat, thinking of her growing up. She would change so much over the weeks, months and years ahead.

So would Grace and Tucker and Nathan.

He realized suddenly and with surprising gratitude that, in some way, Marie Ella would always be a part of his life, but he wondered if he would be around to see the changes that time would bring to the Hopper kids. The insight that he wanted to be there to see them grow stunned him. He could only imagine how much Carissa wanted to see her own children grow up, what it would do to her if Alexandra for some reason gained custody of one or two of them.

No, that could not happen.

*Lord,* he prayed silently, staring down at his wriggly little niece, *please, don't let Carissa be separated from her children. Make the path easier somehow for all of them. She's had enough pain, enough loss, enough difficulty.*

For some reason, he thought of the phone app. They'd just been playing around with it, but could that really turn into something profitable? He went over it in his mind, realizing that he needed to make some phone calls, ask some questions.

A poke in the shoulder made him jump.

"Well?" Petra asked as she took the baby from him.

He blinked at her, wondering when she'd come into the room. "Well what?"

"Weren't you listening?" She hoisted the baby onto her shoulder and began to pat her little back. "Have the aunties said anything about the Fourth of July?"

The aunties often hosted an Independence Day celebration at Chatam House, but with all that had been happening lately, Phillip wondered if it was a good idea this year. Perhaps they were wondering the same thing.

"Uh, with Carissa's dad, uh, that is, Chester's brother, having passed away recently, they may want to curtail activities this year. I'll, um, have to ask them." Someone ought to ask Carissa how she felt about it. She ought to have a say. Chatam House was her home, too, at least for now.

* * *

"So what did you and Phillip talk about before you went to the park today?" Carissa asked as she tucked Nathan into bed beside his brother that evening.

Nathan smoothed the covers and looked away, shrugging. "Oh, he said he wasn't good husband or father material, stuff like that."

Carissa's heart thunked heavily inside her chest, but she kept her gaze bland. It was no more than she'd expected, no more than Phillip had essentially said to her.

"What else?" she probed lightly.

Nathan looked down at his hands. "He said you missed Dad more'n I do and I miss him more'n Tucker and Grace."

"Uh-uh!" Tucker protested, sitting up sleepily.

"Do too!" Nathan insisted. "You don't hardly even remember him."

"I still miss him," Tucker insisted glumly, plopping back on his pillow. "And I think Phillip is good husband and father 'terial."

Carissa straightened the covers. "It doesn't matter," she said briskly. "Now, go to—"

A tap at the door to the suite had her looking into the hallway. Nathan rolled up onto one elbow.

"I bet that's him."

"Go to sleep," she instructed, her heart rate

accelerating as she moved swiftly around the bed and headed out the door, pulling it closed behind her.

She rushed across the sitting room and flung open the outer door, only to be greeted by a mattress. It shifted, so that the narrow end poked through the doorway. She recognized the bunky boards that were part of the boys' bunk beds as Phillip and another man carried them into the suite. She noticed that Phillip clanked as he moved, his pockets full of tools.

"I hope it's not too late," Phillip said, "but when Dale offered to help me move the bunk beds tonight, well, I… Oh, uh, Carissa Hopper, this is my brother-in-law, Dale Bowen. Dale loaned us his truck the other day."

Bowen set down his burden, though Carissa knew from experience that the padded bunky boards, which were composed of a stiff foam board and a foam mattress, were fairly lightweight. He smiled and shook hands with her.

"Thank you, Mr. Bowen."

"Dale," he said, picking up the bunky board again. "Where do you want this?"

"Uh." Carissa pointed toward the bedroom, and Phillip led the way. "They aren't asleep yet, but I'm not sure about—"

Nathan appeared in the hallway. "Oh, boy!" he said. Then, "Tucker, get up!" He motioned for Phillip and Dale Bowen to come ahead with the boards.

Phillip complied, instructing, "Get these tools out of my pockets so we can tear down the big bed."

Nathan worked quickly, running to his room with the tools in his arms. Phillip paused to look at Carissa. "It's okay, isn't it? He really wants his own bed."

"It's okay," she said in a thick voice.

While Phillip dismantled the queen bed, Dale Bowen carried in the pieces of the bunk beds from the landing. Then both men carried the queen bed out, returning to put together the bunks. Dale left at that point, and Phillip went to scrounge up linens, apologizing for not thinking to bring any from the storage unit. Carissa used the sheets from the queen bed to make up the top bunk for Tucker, who was so sleepy that she had to help him climb the ladder into the top bunk. Phillip returned with fresh sheets just as Tucker crawled through the opening in the side of the upper.

"Come on, slide your legs beneath the covers," Carissa coached.

At five feet and five inches in height, she had difficulty at the best of times pulling up the covers, but with so much sheet tucked in, she was finding it nearly impossible. Standing nearly a foot taller than her, Phillip would naturally have an easier time of it.

"Here, let me," he said, passing her the sheets for Nathan's bed. While she shook out Nathan's sheets and began sorting top from bottom, Phillip got Tucker settled. "There you go, buddy. Sleep tight."

Tucker yawned and mumbled, "Good night." Then, with the bedding folded beneath his arms just so and the pillow adjusted beneath his head to his liking, he proclaimed, "See! He is too good father 'terial."

Carissa paused in the act of smoothing the sheet over the mattress of the lower bunk, thankful that the shadow of the upper hid her flaming face from view, while Nathan silently smacked his forehead against the bunk bed's outer foot post. Phillip cleared his throat and backed up a step, his hands sliding into his pockets.

"Well, I'll let y'all…" The words drifted off as he moved toward the door.

Finding her gumption, Carissa straightened and turned to face him. "Thank you, Phillip. The room has much more space now, and the boys will be much happier this way."

"Yes," Nathan said evenly, drawing a deep breath. "I like this much better." He faced Phillip then, balancing his weight on the balls of his feet like a prizefighter, his arms at his sides. Very solemnly, he lifted his hand.

Phillip smiled, just a little, and shook Nathan's hand.

Tears blurred Carissa's eyes. She didn't know why—perhaps because her son was growing up, perhaps because he and Phillip had called a truce, perhaps because it was understood now that Phillip was no threat. Good husband and father material or not, Phillip Chatam had made it clear that he had no interest in becoming either, at least not so far as she and her children were concerned.

"I'll talk to you tomorrow," he said, and Carissa nodded, though she had no intention of talking to him ever again, if she could help it.

She watched him go then tucked in her son once more. Phillip might not think that he was husband or father material, but she knew better. He had been helpful and kind and would be, she had no doubt, until the day that she left this house. But that didn't mean that he could ever feel for her what she wanted him to feel. Therefore, the only sensible thing she could do was keep her distance—and hope that would be enough to protect her needy children and her own foolish heart.

# *Chapter Eleven*

Over the next few days, as June wound to its inevitable close, Carissa did everything she could to avoid Phillip. She stayed in her suite as much as possible and kept the children with her, coaching them to answer the door and say that Mom was too busy to speak with anyone who stopped by. It helped that the boys were happy to play in their new bedroom, now that they had more space, and that a case of the sniffles kept Grace confined for a bit. They took all of their meals in their suite, too, but one thing she could not avoid was laundry.

It seemed that she and the children had a load of laundry to do every other day, but at least she didn't have to drive down to the coin laundry and dump her hard-earned cash into a bank of machines. Instead, she carried each load to the dumbwaiter and sent it down to the butler's pantry off the kitchen. Then she would tote it the short distance to the laundry room behind the pantry. After sending the loaded laundry basket down in the dumbwaiter as usual, Carissa tiptoed along the landing then craned her neck to look over into the stairwell. She saw that it was empty, so she moved quickly down the stairs that led to the foyer. A quick glance around the curve showed her that the way was clear.

Reaching the bottom of the stairs, Carissa ran light-footedly into the butler's pantry. No sooner did she open the door to the dumbwaiter than Hilda stuck her head into the room from the kitchen.

"There you are! The Misses want to see you in the parlor."

Carissa started and gulped. "The Misses? Oh, you mean the Chatam sisters. What do they want with me?"

Hilda nodded. "They want you to join them for tea. Go on now. I just took in the tray."

Carissa gestured at the basket of laundry. "But I need to—"

Hilda waved a hand dismissively. "Oh, I'll put that in the washer. You can shift it later. Meanwhile, Chester will go up and sit with the children."

Carissa couldn't very well argue. Her hostesses had asked very little in return for their hospitality. Still, she sensed that this was something more than a friendly tea party.

"Cold water is fine," she muttered, tucking wisps of hair behind her ears. She smoothed the wrinkles from her faded purple T-shirt and wished the hems of her jeans were not so frayed as she sauntered back down the hallway in her worn canvas slip-ons.

Odelia and Kent met her just inside the parlor. Garbed in another outrageous costume, Odelia flitted and fluttered like the origami hummingbirds hanging by delicate springs from her earlobes, the iridescent fabric of her ensemble seeming to have a life of its own. Kent, meanwhile, resembled a plump barber pole encased in a white suit. Carissa couldn't help smiling. Her smile died, however, when she saw that Phillip was also in attendance.

He stood with one elbow propped against the edge of the ornate white plaster mantel above the fireplace, looking cool, calm, collected and more handsome than a man had a right to be in khakis and a blue-gray shirt, the sleeves rolled up to display his tanned, corded forearms. His tight smile displayed his dimples and seemed to dare her to try to escape. Any hope that he hadn't realized she'd been purposefully avoiding him promptly vanished.

She switched her gaze to his aunts, putting on

a polite smile as Odelia, supported by her husband's arm, dropped down on the brocade settee. Hypatia, sitting on a gold-on-gold-striped chair, waved Carissa forward while Magnolia poured a cup of tea from the gleaming silver pot on the tray in the middle of the low, oblong piecrust table. Magnolia placed the delicate china cup on a matching saucer, added a spoon, picked up a thick cloth napkin and passed everything to Carissa when she came within reach.

"Take that chair, dear," Hypatia directed, indicating the armless chair beside the fireplace. Kent seated himself beside Odelia just as she leaned forward and slid a small tray of condiments to the end of the table nearest Carissa, who took the opportunity to add a bit of honey and lemon to her cup before sliding back into her seat. She stirred, rested the spoon on the saucer, lifted her cup and sipped.

All three Chatam sisters seemed to be perched on the edges of their seats. Carissa felt that she had to say something.

"Mmm. Very good."

The sisters relaxed with pleased smiles.

Carissa sipped again and wished that she could relax, too, but Phillip hovered over her like a giant bird of prey. She wondered what was coming and began mentally recalculating the estimate she'd recently made of how soon she would be ready to move out on her own. She was so busy revising her budget that she almost completely missed Hypatia's opening gambit and had to ask her to repeat herself.

"I beg your pardon? What did you say?"

"I said, dear, that it's almost Independence Day."

"Oh. Yes, I suppose it is."

"We here at Chatam House do so enjoy a good Independence Day celebration," Odelia gushed.

"The children would enjoy the parade, I'm sure," Kent put in. "That is, if you think it's appropriate."

Carissa smiled, wondering why an Independence Day parade might be considered inappropriate. "Certainly," she said lamely, wondering where this was going.

"We were thinking of a barbecue this year," Magnolia said, "to show off the pool, you know." She smiled at Kent, nodding in his direction.

"But perhaps a small party would be best," Hypatia ventured, "all things considered."

Carissa blinked at her, getting the feeling that "all things" depended heavily upon her.

"What my aunts are trying to say," Phillip told her, "is that though they usually host a large Independence Day celebration, out of concern for you and your children, they are willing to cut back or even cancel the event this year, although canceling at this late date would be difficult."

Carissa twisted around in her chair to gape at him. "Out of concern for *us?* I—I don't understand."

"Well, of course you don't," he snapped. "You've gone out of your way to avoid contact with everyone in this house! I've been trying to talk to you about this for days."

"I haven't... We..." She gulped and looked away. "I don't know what *we* have to do with the Chatam Independence Day celebration."

"The year Daddy died, we weren't in the mood for a party for months," Magnolia revealed softly.

"Oh," Carissa breathed, as understanding dawned at last.

"Now, we have spoken to Chester and Hilda," Hypatia said briskly, "and their only concern is for you and the children."

Astonished at the kindness and consideration of these sweet ladies, Carissa quickly said, "We wouldn't dream of curtailing your celebration plans."

"Are you sure, dear?" Odelia asked. "It won't bring back bittersweet memories of celebrations past for you or the children?"

Carissa shook her head adamantly. Her children had seldom enjoyed a real Independence Day celebration. "In fact, I think it might be good for us. You know, take our minds off…" She resisted the urge to glance at Phillip, finishing meekly with "things."

The sisters traded satisfied smiles, then to Carissa's chagrin, they looked to Phillip as if for final approval. He cleared his throat and said, "Well, if she's sure, I guess we carry on as planned."

"There's just one other thing, dear," Hypatia said, smiling benignly at Carissa.

"What's that, ma'am?"

"My sisters and I are wondering where you and the children plan to attend church. We've noticed that you haven't been going with Chester and Hilda, and we thought you might prefer to attend Downtown Bible Church with us. Of course, if you have somewhere else in mind, that's fine, too."

Carissa got the message loud and clear. As long as she lived in their home, these ladies expected her and her children to attend church. It was very little to ask, considering their generosity.

"Actually," Carissa said smoothly, "we quite like Uncle Chester and Aunt Hilda's church."

"Oh," Odelia said, giving the word several syllables and sounding disappointed.

"Your troubles are bound to seem lighter

once you get back into the habit of regular attendance," Magnolia stated kindly.

Carissa had thought something similar herself, and she wasn't about to argue the point. She did argue when the topic turned to meals. Perhaps she shouldn't have, but Carissa continued to insist that she and the children take dinner in their suite.

For one thing, she and the children simply didn't have the clothes to wear to the Chatam table every evening. They barely had appropriate clothing to wear to church. For another, the children were tired and not at their best by dinnertime. Often, they needed baths before they could eat, and afterward it was most convenient to dress them in their pajamas. She compromised by agreeing to go downstairs for breakfast in the sunroom and take lunch in the kitchen to make things easier on Hilda.

With that settled, she smiled and sipped her tea as talk moved to plans for Independence Day. When her cup was empty, she declined another, set the saucer down, excused herself and went out to check on her children and her laundry. She felt Phillip's eyes on her as she left the room, but he did not follow, and in the days ahead, he kept his distance, merely nodding when they passed on the upstairs landing or in the downstairs hallways, and did not appear at breakfast.

It was absurd to feel hurt, of course. She had started this game, but Phillip's absence left a gaping hole in her life. Somehow, despite her better judgment and best intentions, she had become dependent on him in a dozen little ways, and they all added up to a significant presence that no longer was, had never really been and would never be. The children felt it, too, and all of their lives seemed a little less bright because of it. But they had lived with loss in one shape or another for a very long time; Carissa told herself that they would adjust.

She did what she always did—she kept on keeping on, and soon Independence Day arrived. Independence Day meant putting aside work and joining in the celebration, being part of the whole Chatam family for the day. It also meant pulling out the red, white and blue bits of their respective wardrobes to make a properly patriotic display.

The kids got into the spirit right away. Grace wore a ruffled red knit sundress that was too small for her over a pair of white shorts and white sandals. Carissa used a long, white, filmy scarf to tie a big, floppy bow around Grace's soft red hair, above her right ear. Nathan chose a red-and-white-striped shirt, jeans cut off at the knee and blue canvas shoes, while Tucker went all red: T-shirt, shorts, socks and shoes. The left shoe had a hole in the toe.

In a flash of creativity born of desperation, Carissa cut a star out of the denim shorn from Nathan's too-short jeans and glued it over the hole in the toe of Tucker's shoe. The kids were so impressed that she wound up having to glue blue denim stars to their shoes, too. She even hand sewed them to the straps of Grace's sundress top to make them longer so the dress didn't bind the child under the arms.

For herself, Carissa made do with her good white blouse, blue jeans and freshly laundered white canvas shoes, tying her hair up on top of her head in a ponytail with a red bandanna. Half of her hair promptly flopped about her face in wisps and tendrils, but she left it, tucking what she could behind her ears, and hurried the children downstairs to breakfast.

She sensed Phillip's presence even before she entered the sunroom. He sat at a table with Hypatia and Magnolia, drinking black coffee and eating a mound of pancakes topped by blueberries, strawberries and whipped cream. Grace ran straight to him, but after a single glance of acknowledgment in Carissa's direction, he seemed content to ignore her, even as he lifted Grace into the chair at his side, filled her plate, tucked a napkin under her chin and proceeded to oversee her breakfast.

Carissa made sure that Grace had milk to

drink and didn't use too much syrup, but she might as well have been invisible so far as Phillip Chatam was concerned. He had eyes and ears only for Grace and his aunties. For them he was all easy smiles.

Meanwhile, Carissa seated the boys at another table, filled plates and glasses for them and made certain that no more than an adequate supply of syrup flooded their pancakes before cutting them into bite-size pieces. Phillip finished his breakfast and rose just about the same time that Odelia and Kent arrived, decked out in eye-popping patriotic finery.

Kent sported a white straw hat, a white linen suit and a red shirt worn with a blue vest decorated with palm-sized white stars. Beside him, Odelia dripped white sequined stars of all sizes from her flowing red dress to her blue sandals and sash. She wore them attached to the brim of a red, wide-brimmed straw hat and dangled them from her earlobes in long chains, and stars the size of saucers fixed the sash at her waist and shoulder. The boys literally hooted when the pair of them came into the room, and Grace stood in her chair to applaud.

Phillip picked up his plate to clear his place, but Odelia and Kent went to join the boys. Shaking his head, Phillip headed off to the kitchen via the butler's pantry, remarking to the room in general that he'd see everyone later. Carissa took his place, filling her plate from the sideboard that Hilda had stocked at some point.

She told herself that she was relieved to have him out of the room, but deep down she felt a bit slighted…wounded, even, the truth be told, which was nonsense. The man was much too handsome for her own good, and while he might be kind and thoughtful and instinctively adept with the children, he lacked ambition and discipline, by his own admission. The wisest thing she could do was to keep her distance.

She managed to do that for another three hours or so, walking with the Chatam sisters and her aunt and uncle down to the corner of the estate to watch the Independence Day parade as it wound its way through the historic district from the downtown square of Buffalo Creek. As soon as they returned to the house, however, the place began to fill up with people, and Phillip seemed always to be at hand, greeting the newcomers with hugs and smiles and making quick introductions. The first to arrive were Garrett and Jessa Willows and their son, Hunter, all of whom promptly swept Carissa's children outside to play. Garrett, the former Chatam gardener, promised to show them all the secret places on the estate.

Before Carissa could catch her breath, she met more Chatams than she'd known existed, starting with Asher and his wife, Ellie, and their baby daughter, Marie Ella. Next came Petra and her husband, Dale Bowen, whom she'd met the other night, followed quickly by Reeves and Anna Leland and their daughter, Gilli. Reeves's sister Melinda and her husband, J. W. Harris, came with their little boy, Johnny. To everyone else's surprise, Reeves and Melinda's twin baby sisters, Harmony and Lyric, showed up, too, saying they were just passing through on their way home to California after visiting friends in New York.

While the Chatam sisters were getting their nieces settled upstairs, Kaylie breezed in with her husband, the hockey player Stephen Gallow, and her father, Hub Chatam, who led the grief support group. Kaylie's brother, Chandler, arrived from Stephenville with his wife, Bethany, and their little son, Matthew. Another of her brothers, a much older one, Bayard Chatam, and his wife, Chloe, brought along their married daughter Julia and her sons Richard Paul and Brian Travis, their father being out of town on business. Bayard promised that his younger daughters would be along later, and one of them, Carolyn, arrived on the arm of her uncle Morgan, a distinguished-looking college professor and Kaylie's second-oldest brother.

Then Carissa met Phillip's parents, who arrived with Dallas. Thereafter, Phillip never again left Carissa's side, a circumstance for which she quickly became thankful, given that the Drs. Murdock and Maryanne Chatam made a formidable pair and seemed to have a particular interest in her.

Dr. Murdock Chatam stood tall and straight, with a head of thick, graying hair, cinnamon-brown eyes and a patrician profile, complete with the Chatam cleft chin. Dr. Maryanne Chatam was slender and of average height, with blond, silver-streaked hair cut in a stylish bob and gray-blue eyes as sharp as scalpels, especially when they honed in on Carissa, which they did the instant that Dallas made the introduction.

"My daughter tells me you have three children," said Maryanne.

"*And* that she's a widow, no doubt," Phillip added, stepping up to Carissa's side, "*and* that her father recently passed *and* that she's a whiz with computers and any number of other things, I'm sure."

"Including that she's Chester's niece and is staying here at Chatam House," his father stated in weighty tones.

"And now we're all up to date on Carissa Hopper," Phillip said, taking her by the arm and aiming a very pointed look at his sister. Dallas shrugged and shook her head defensively as Phillip maneuvered Carissa away and escorted her quickly through the house and out onto the patio, which was crawling with people.

"What was that about?" Carissa asked once they were well away from his parents.

"My meddling sister," Phillip said between his teeth.

"I don't understand."

"Dallas has a penchant for...interfering," he told her, "but don't worry. I won't let my parents grill you."

"Why would they do that?"

He huffed out a breath. "Let me restate. Dallas has a penchant for *matchmaking*. She nearly burned down Kent's house while trying to get him and Aunt Odelia together. And managed to spark a romance between Asher and Ellie in the process. She almost derailed Petra and Dale, however, and after that near fiasco, she supposedly reformed. But now here she is with our parents, and they've got their sights on you, which tells me that someone's been talking you up."

Carissa caught her breath, blinking. "You're saying that Dallas thinks you and I should be a couple."

"And my parents will almost certainly oppose it," he confirmed with a nod.

Carissa frowned. "But why?"

He shrugged. "Because they oppose everything I do, that's why."

"I don't understand."

"Oh, it's very simple. Asher is the responsible elder son. I'm the irresponsible younger one."

"Okay, you don't have a job right now, but that will change. Won't it?"

"Eventually it has to," he said offhandedly, "but let's go over some of the jobs I've already had. I've taught surfing and snowboarding. I've fished in Alaska. Briefly. It wasn't as fun as it looked. Oh, and I've fed lions in a zoo."

"Lions!"

"Elephants, too. Different zoo." He waved that away. "What else? There was skydiving. You'd be amazed how many people want to jump out of airplanes. I led treks in the Canadian Northwest. And in between the grand adventures there was making sails, stenciling boats, tanning alligator hides, selling everything from books to jewelry, modeling kilts."

"Modeling—"

"And I even made a credible barista. Oh, and I did work on a play and for a band, at one time, but that was way back, when I was first in college and thought I might actually make a career in something. Out of all that, I don't think I've ever had one job that my parents actually approved of, though. Or one girlfriend."

"And they think *I'm* your girlfriend?"

"Something like that."

"Well, then, we'll just set them straight."

"Oh, sure," he said flippantly, "because that's always worked so well for me in the past. Just leave it to me, will you? I'm an expert at putting up a wall between me and the Doctors Chatam," he assured her, waving at his brother-in-law and another couple. "Just stay close. Unless you want to be probed."

Sure, that was just what she needed. And what would she say if his parents asked her outright if she wanted to be with their son? That she didn't know what she wanted?

"I'll leave it to you," she muttered, her head swirling.

"Smart girl."

Carissa soon met Dale Bowen's sister and her husband, as well as a number of other young parents. Her cousins arrived with their children, much to the delight of Hilda and Chester. Meanwhile, her own children were having the time of their lives, running and playing with the other kids in attendance.

Nathan, as usual, was the gang leader, but Gilli Leland was giving him a run for his money. A bossy little thing, she had him hopping, justifying his every order and suggestion, much to Grace's giggling delight. Tucker and Hunter Willows, meanwhile, had become fast friends. The others were barely big enough to join in, but

Nathan, Gilli and Grace were good about seeing to it that they were included, and the other parents shared in keeping an eye on everyone.

Carissa relaxed a bit, even with the Doctors Chatam observing from a distance and Phillip glued to her side. Or maybe it was *because* he was at her side. Even with all the couples around her, for once, she didn't feel out of place, an oddity. It was almost as if she and Phillip were a couple, at least for the moment.

Oh, he didn't do anything to especially make it seem that way, behaving exactly as a casual friend might, but he was there when she would otherwise have been alone in a group of young couples. Perhaps the assumption by his parents, and maybe even the assumptions of others, fed the feeling.

Or maybe she just wanted to be a part of a couple so badly that she couldn't help feeling part of a pair.

For whatever reason, she let it be. For one day. That wasn't chancing too much. Or was it?

She thought over all that he'd told her, all that he'd done, flitting from one interesting occupation to another, doing whatever job took his fancy. She understood what he was waiting for now. He was cooling his heels until the next big thing came along, until a fun job or an exciting adventure presented itself. Meanwhile, he'd amuse himself with her and her kids.

On one hand, she ought to be grateful. He'd been so much help. On the other hand, she wanted to shake him. Didn't he realize what he was doing? He was making her—them—fall in love with him, when he had no intention of staying around. Even knowing that he would take off as soon as the next great challenge came along, she couldn't quite seem to help herself, and her poor children had absolutely no defenses against a man like him. They weren't used to a man who spent time with them and showed affection to them. Even Nathan was at risk.

But what could she do? Berate the man for being kind? She'd tried to keep her distance, and that hadn't worked.

She felt helpless. All she could do was tell herself over and over again that it was just for one day. Just one day.

Just one day to enjoy being with Phillip Chatam.

But it wasn't enough.

# *Chapter Twelve*

Several portable grills had been set up along one end of the patio, and when the steaks, hamburgers and hot dogs came out, Phillip did his part, along with Asher, Garrett, Chester, Dale and Chandler, in cooking the meat. Meanwhile, Carissa helped Hilda and the other ladies lay out a spread that consisted of half-a-dozen enormous salads, a variety of chips and dips, baked beans, a wide selection of condiments, a bushel basket of corn on the cob and many other dishes. What thrilled the children most were the cakes and the three large electric ice-cream makers that sat humming beneath one table. Periodically, either Hilda or Chester would add crushed ice and rock salt to the outer containers while the cylinder turned inside.

The steaks started coming off the grills about midafternoon, much to the delight of the very hungry crowd. Despite having grazed their way through mountains of chips and bowls of dip and other goodies, many had worked up appetites in the pool or playing games of horseshoes or badminton on the lawn. Carissa didn't have a bathing suit, so she'd declined to swim and instead had partnered Phillip in a winning game of badminton before claiming a spot beside him at one of the tables on the patio and chatting with Jessa and Garrett Willows.

Somehow, they got on the subject of phone apps, and Garrett asked about the possibility of designing an app that would allow a customer to take a photo of a plant and identify it. Carissa promised to investigate the possibility and was shocked, pleasantly so, at Phillip's easy comment.

"If anyone can figure it out, Carissa can. She's a computer genius." She nearly spun her head off her neck goggling at him, but he just smiled and went on. "Maybe when we're through with our current project, we can look into yours in more detail."

*Our current project.* Carissa cleared her throat and ducked her head. Maybe she shouldn't have avoided him these past several days. Maybe, if they worked together, he would see her as more than a lull in the series of adventures that was his life. She told herself not to be a loon, but keeping her distance hadn't worked, so why not take a chance on spending a little time with him? She closed her eyes and took a deep breath.

*All right, Lord, here goes nothing.*

"Maybe, um, we can work on the project Saturday evening after I put the kids to bed," she suggested to Phillip softly.

He looked down at her. "I thought you might be working Saturday to make up for today," he replied evasively.

"Well, yes, but not so late into the evening."

"You have to have some downtime," he said. He shifted forward then, enthusiasm lighting his eyes as he went on. "I've been making some phone calls, though, talking to people who might be interested in the kind of application we're considering, and so far the feedback has been very positive."

Phillip's sister Petra came over then and whispered into his ear, but Carissa couldn't help overhearing.

"I just wanted to apologize. It was Ellie who, um, spilled the beans to our parents, so to speak, but really, it only took a remark that you had mentioned..." She glanced at Carissa. "...a certain someone."

"And Mom and Dad were all over it," Phillip surmised, straightening. "But if Ellie made the initial remark, then why are *you* apologizing?"

"Well," Petra drawled, glancing at Carissa again, "after Mom couldn't get anywhere with Dallas, she called me, and eventually—I emphasize *eventually*—I told her everything I knew. Honestly, Phil, she was like a dog with a bone."

Carissa watched as Phillip's mouth compressed into a tight line, but then he sighed, patted his sister's hand and pushed back his chair.

"I have to go make an apology now," Phillip said. Petra nodded in obvious understanding as he rose. "Stay with Carissa until I get back, will you?" Again, Petra nodded.

Carissa started to say, "Oh, that's not necessary," but Petra cut her off before she got the last word fully out.

"But I want to." She settled into Phillip's chair as he strode off in the direction of his baby sister. "I've been wanting to get to know you better."

"Oh? That's, uh, nice."

Petra laughed. "You must think we're terrible."

"Why, no," Carissa hedged uncomfortably. "Why would I?"

"It's just that Mom and Dad have such high expectations, you see," Petra explained kindly. "You should have seen what they put Dale through last year before we married. Now, of course, he's perfect, as least so far as they're concerned. And Ellie. Oh, my. They adore her. After all, she's the mother of their first grandchild, but you should see the look on Dad's face even now whenever Ash talks about the practice uniforms that she devised for her soccer team."

Petra launched into a comical description of floppy ears attached to caps and tutus worn over shorts. Garrett Willows joined in to explain how Ellie had used those things to teach the children on her team proper running and kicking techniques. Carissa didn't have the faintest idea what it was all about, but she couldn't help laughing at the vivid pictures they painted. Phillip returned and sent his sister off with hugs. She patted Carissa's shoulder as she left them.

"Nice talking to you."

"You, too."

As soon as Petra disappeared into the crowd, Carissa leaned close to Phillip and asked, "Everything okay with Dallas?"

"Yeah, I think so."

Before he could elaborate, however, Hubner Chatam stood up and asked for everyone's attention. In short order, Stephen and Kaylie Gallow happily announced that they were expecting their first child in five months' time. What had been a holiday party quickly turned into a true family celebration as everyone rushed to congratulate the beaming young couple. Carissa noted how carefully tall, blond Stephen enfolded Kaylie in his long arms, her back to his chest, as the family gathered around them. Phillip hurried to join the rest of the family, his smile as wide as his face. Carissa couldn't help smiling herself, especially when Hub asked everyone to link hands to join in prayer and Phillip came immediately to snag her hand in his and pull her into the circle.

She felt a great sense of belonging, standing there among all those Chatams, one hand in Phillip's, the other clasped by Jessa, as Hub asked for God's blessing on the new baby growing in his daughter's womb. It seemed to Carissa that Chatam House must be a blessed place, and she thanked God for the sanctuary she had found there. For however long it lasted.

The afternoon passed into evening without further incident, the awful heat driving many indoors and others to the pool. Carissa allowed the children to swim with Phillip while she sat with her feet dangling in the water. Later, the children pulled their clothes on over their bathing suits and gathered with everyone else to watch the fireworks.

Every Independence Day, the city of Buffalo Creek produced a fireworks extravaganza at the high school football stadium, but not many of the Chatams' guests left to attend. Instead, they dragged lawn chairs out to the west lawn and spread blankets in front of the great magnolia tree to watch from afar as the fireworks painted the night sky with bursts of color.

Phillip spread a blanket between his brother Asher's and that of the Willows family, while Carissa herded her weary children into place. Grace crawled into Phillip's lap and was well on her way to sleep when the first explosion of colored lights lit the sky. Even Nathan seemed too tired to complain, contenting himself with grumbles about the hardness of the ground and the lack of space, but he soon quieted, lying back and folding his hands behind his head to gaze upward with awe at the display. Even with the loud booming of the fireworks, Tucker went to sleep nestled against his mother's side.

Carissa couldn't help stroking his scraggly mop. The boy needed a haircut. She'd have to get out her scissors and make him hold still for it soon. Nathan hated unruly hair and insisted that she keep him trimmed, but if Tucker had his way, he'd be sitting on his hair before he'd sit still for a haircut. She chuckled, thinking that he'd probably use it to swing from the chandeliers.

Phillip looked over, smiled and asked, "What's so funny?"

She shook her head. "Just thinking how strange it is that children with the same parents and raised in the same household can be so different."

He nodded. "I know what you mean. Just

look at me and Ash. There's no more responsible human being on the face of the earth than my big brother." He glanced fondly at Asher then shook his head. "But me...I've always jumped from one interesting job to another, living for myself and no one else."

She schooled her expression to blandness, stroking Tucker's hair. There was the death knell to any foolish dream she might be hiding in her traitorous heart. Why couldn't she listen and take heed?

"Well, at least you've had an interesting life."

Phillip shrugged and looked down at Grace, whose droopy eyes testified to her difficulty staying awake for the fireworks. "It's made for a lonely life at times. I'm just realizing how lonely."

Carissa glanced around at the plethora of Chatams spread over the lawn. "That doesn't seem to be a problem now that you're here."

He grinned. "That's true. Chatam House is the heart of the family. When you're here, you don't lack for company. Or support."

She could see that was true, and she envied him. Her dad and her uncle Chester and aunt Hilda had been the only ones she could ever truly count on in a time of need. Her mother looked out for herself and no one else, and her sister... Only God knew where Lyla was and what she might be doing. Her cousins cared about her, of course, but they had their own responsibilities and difficulties. She wouldn't dream of going to them for help, but Phillip could reach out to almost anyone here tonight, and Carissa had no doubt that they would do their best to help him. They would, in fact, gather round to help him. Yes, she envied Phillip and all the Chatams. No wonder Chester and Hilda were so devoted to them.

The fireworks ended with a breathtaking display of sparkling excess that had Grace sitting up and clapping her hands. Tucker roused and rubbed his eyes, breathing, "Wow!" Even Nathan sat up in silent appreciation.

The last sparks were still fading from the sky as the party finally broke up, with parents carting off sleepy children. The Chatam sisters and Kent stood on the walk in front of the house, saying goodbye to their guests, while Chester and some of the other men took charge of the blankets and chairs. To the sisters' surprise, Phillip's parents declined to stay at Chatam House, choosing instead to sleep under the same roof as their grandbaby. Carissa couldn't help feeling a bit of relief at that.

Phillip insisted on carrying Grace up to her room. He even went in to gently bully Tucker into his pajamas while Carissa got Grace into her nightgown. For once, Nathan didn't complain. Instead, he went into the bathroom and brushed his teeth then changed his clothes and crawled into bed while Carissa and Phillip helped Grace and Tucker brush. Later, when all the children were tucked into bed, Carissa walked Phillip to the door of their suite.

"Thanks for your help."

"No problem. They were so tired."

"They had a wonderful day, and so did I."

"I'm glad."

He smiled down at her, and she stepped closer. She couldn't help herself. A warm feeling flooded her, and she felt certain that he would kiss her. His copper gaze skimmed her face and came to rest on her lips. Her breath caught in anticipation. She shifted her weight to her toes, ready to rise up to meet him. But then he eased back and turned the doorknob. The door opened a few inches.

"If, um, you should change your mind about attending church with the aunties and me on Sunday…"

Disappointment dealt her a crushing blow, but she managed to keep her chin aloft. "I've already told Uncle Chester and Aunt Hilda we'll be going with them."

"All right, then."

"About Saturday night, though…"

"Oh, um, I'm not sure. With my parents here and everything… I'll try, though. I would like to get to work on the app."

"Yes. The app."

"Well, good night."

"Good night."

He slipped out and closed the door behind him. She tried very hard not to cry. She kept telling herself it was for the best. He wasn't the man for her. No good could come from putting herself in Phillip Chatam's way more than necessary. But she didn't have to be happy about it, did she? Besides, he'd said he would try to come by on Saturday night so they could work on the smartphone app. And who knew what might come of that?

Phillip didn't show up on Saturday evening. He hadn't actually said he would, of course, and Carissa tried to convince herself that she hadn't believed he would, but she couldn't help feeling disappointed and foolish. Glad that she'd decided to attend church the next morning with Chester and Hilda, she consoled herself with the idea that she wouldn't have to face him. She prayed herself to sleep that night; it was that or cry again.

The children complained about getting up early the next morning, but they were happy enough by the time they piled into the vehicle with Chester and Hilda. They all went together in Carissa's minivan, with Chester doing the driving, Aunt Hilda riding up front in the passenger seat and Carissa sitting in the bucket seat next to Grace. That left the boys to share the third-row bench in the back.

As Carissa slid the door closed, Grace looked around and asked, "Where's Phillip?"

Carissa's heart did a little flip. Had he become such a part of their lives, then, in spite of everything? She managed a smile and said, "He's going to church with his aunties."

"Oh," Grace said confidently. "He's saving us our seats."

"Uh, no," Carissa told her. "He and the aunties go to a different church."

"Oh." Grace imbued that one word with a wealth of disappointment and sadness.

Carissa said nothing more, just fastened her seat belt and faced forward.

Chester drove them across town to the small, unprepossessing church where he and Hilda had worshipped for decades.

Buffalo Creek Christian Church was as plain inside as out, but the small congregation could not have been more welcoming or warm. A simple piano and a single guitar provided the music. A mixed quartet took the place of a big, robed choir. There were no media productions, but the worship was sincere and deep, and the pastor's message hit Carissa squarely in the chest.

The theme of the sermon, taken from the fourth chapter of Philippians, was that God supplied all our needs "according to the riches of His glory." Carissa had to admit that her needs had been met, albeit in ways she had not foreseen. She trusted that would continue, somehow.

When they arrived back at Chatam House, Carissa was surprised to see Phillip and Kent carrying in large quantities of fried chicken and all the fixings. Chester chuckled when Kent called out that there was plenty for him and Hilda, too. Chester and Hilda always had Sundays off, and the household fended for themselves. The Chatam sisters had repeatedly invited Carissa and the children to join them for Sunday meals, while reiterating that they "ate simple," out of deference for the Lord's Day, but Carissa had always taken the children out for fast food or managed a simple meal on her own. Today, however, Phillip made it clear that they were expected to join everyone else at the table.

"After the Independence Day celebration, the aunties feel that everyone deserves a break from meal preparation, so today we ordered in." He lifted the bags, wafting the aroma of fried chicken on the July air. "Now, who wants a chicken leg?"

Grace immediately started hopping up and down. "I do! I do!"

Carissa sighed, knowing she couldn't refuse without risking a rebellion. Even Nathan was licking his chops. "All three of you had better be on your best behavior at the table."

Tucker and Nathan both ran for the front door. Phillip grinned and winked at Carissa. "We ordered a chicken with six legs."

She laughed. "That's a critter I'd like to see around the barnyard."

"I prefer 'em all crispy and brown, dressing the dinner table," Phillip joked, falling into step beside her as she followed the children.

She laughed again, relieved that no one seemed to be avoiding anyone anymore. Maybe he'd just been too busy to stop by on Saturday. No doubt he'd been obligated to spend time with his parents. Besides, it was just business, nothing personal. That was what she had to remember.

They went into the house. Phillip carried the food to the kitchen, while Carissa hurried the children into the dining room. Odelia and Kent were putting plates on the table, and they immediately deputized the children to lay out silverware and napkins, sending Carissa after drinking glasses. Meanwhile, Hypatia, Magnolia and Phillip transferred the food to serving dishes.

Chester and Hilda elected to take their meal

to the carriage house, but everyone else gathered around the dark antique table in the old-fashioned formal dining room. High spirits prevailed. The Independence Day celebration coupled with Kaylie and Stephen's happy announcement had created a gay atmosphere among the Chatam sisters. Odelia had even dressed for the occasion in shades of pastel pink and blue, going so far as to wear one pink rosebud earring and one bluebell earring. Grace thought the earrings were adorable and kept checking out Odelia's earlobes, vacillating between favorites. She finally decided on the pink rosebud because, in her words, "Blue is for stinky boys."

"Hey!" Phillip teased. "I'll have you know that I had a shower before church this morning."

Grace erupted in giggles. "You're not a boy! You're a daddy."

Phillip almost dropped his fork. Carissa felt her face heat, and throats cleared all around the table, while Nathan rolled his eyes before saying, "He's not a daddy. He's just a man."

Phillip nodded stiffly and dropped his gaze to his plate. "That's right," he said. "I'm just a man."

Carissa rushed to fill the awkward silence with chatter. "Not all adult men are fathers, Grace. In fact, many are not, just as many adult women are not mothers."

"None of us are mothers," Hypatia pointed out, indicating herself and her sisters.

"We've always been content as sisters and aunties," Magnolia said matter-of-factly.

"Except for me," Odelia put in, squeezing Kent's hand. "I'm also a wife."

"But not a mother," Grace mused, sounding puzzled.

"Not a mother," Odelia said a tad wistfully. "I'm a step-grandmother, though, and great-aunt."

Grace just blinked and shook her head at that. Amused at herself, she began making goofy sounds. Tucker joined in, rolling his eyes and wagging his tongue. Carissa attempted to control them, but Grace's giggles proved infectious, and soon everyone was laughing—everyone, Carissa noticed, except Phillip. He managed a smile, but his heart didn't seem in it. She wanted to squeeze his hand, as Odelia had squeezed Kent's earlier, but she didn't dare. Not when her heart reached out for his every time he was near.

*He's just a man. Just a man.*

Phillip had never felt so inconsequential, so pointless. Living in the same house with Carissa and her children was becoming more and more difficult. He felt constantly torn between seeking her out and avoiding her, between drawing her closer and keeping her at a distance. He felt drawn to her in a way that he'd never felt drawn to another woman, but he was painfully aware that he had nothing to offer her, not even a steady income. All his experience amounted to a lot of memories, some of them great fun and some of them not so pleasant, and yet he didn't know how to remake himself.

Oh, his parents had ideas about that. They'd made those notions plain when he'd seen them at Asher's on Friday and again when they'd taken him to dinner on Saturday. His dad had urged him to study for his CPA license, but Phillip didn't have the constitution to become a Certified Public Accountant. He would hate a job that made him sit in an office day in and day out, doing the same routine tasks. It just wasn't for him. His mother thought he should try for a teaching certificate, of all things, but Phillip could not imagine himself with a classroom full of Nathans or, worse yet, Tuckers. The idea of willingly walking into a classroom full of kids every day gave him the willies. He felt a new respect for his baby sister just thinking about it.

His mother had baldly accused Carissa of pegging him as her next husband, saying that it was understandable why a penniless widow with three children to raise would target a single man from a good family. Phillip had laughed at the idea. Maybe Carissa didn't hate him, maybe she even liked him, as Nathan assumed, but she certainly hadn't *targeted* him. If she had, Phillip didn't want to think how susceptible he might actually be to any lures that Carissa should cast his way, though what she'd want with him was a mystery. She needed a husband who could help her provide for her children, not an overgrown playmate for them.

If only they could make something of the smartphone app, he might cast some lures of his own. She could do worse than a Chatam, after all, even an irresponsible, self-indulgent one, for once she was part of the family, she would have all the support and help anyone could ever need.

The problem with the app came down to public interest, though. He didn't doubt that Carissa had the know-how to make the thing work, and he had all the contacts. His former employer and coworkers were all surprisingly enthusiastic about the possibilities. In fact, his previous boss had gone so far as to predict that streaming a climb live or on video would increase business by double digits, induce their clients to be better behaved and foster a greater sense of caution in everyone involved. The guy was so enthusiastic that he was talking it up to his suppliers and offering to underwrite a portion of the project. No, the one real unknown was whether the general public would show any interest in watching a climb in real time or on video. Only God knew the answer to that. As Phillip pondered the possibilities, he remembered a couple of points from that morning's sermon at Downtown Bible Church.

"Every experience is part of God's divine plan for you," the pastor had said. "Maybe you've made mistakes, but mistakes are proof that you're trying, and God's plan is bigger than your mistakes, so wherever you are now, that's where God wants you at this moment."

And where he was, at the moment, Phillip mused, was living in the same house with a woman who could very well make the smartphone app a reality, a woman who made him want to be more than he ever had been. If they could pull this off together, maybe they had a chance for something more. Maybe Carissa would begin to look at him as more than a friend to whom she owed her gratitude.

Even if that never happened, however, the successful development of the app could benefit her and the kids financially, and they needed it. Maybe he could give them that, at least. Phillip closed his eyes and sent up a silent prayer for Carissa and the kids. They had to come first. His wants hardly mattered next to their needs.

Maybe he was just a man, but it was time that

he became the best man he could be, time that he thought of someone besides himself, so he swallowed the truth of the matter, put on a smile and made himself enjoy the remainder of the meal.

He found much to enjoy. The food wasn't as good as Hilda's, but the company couldn't be faulted. His aunties practically glowed, they were so thrilled for his cousin Kaylie and her husband, Stephen. Phillip had never thought much about babies before, but his little niece had gotten him to thinking. Ash and Ellie were so proud of her, so enchanted by her.

Phillip couldn't help comparing Marie Ella to Grace, wondering if she would one day be as charming and sweet. It didn't seem possible. Already their personalities seemed so different. He wondered how different Tucker and Nathan might have been as babies. Had Nathan been solemn and knowing even as an infant? Did Tucker always have that sparkle in his eyes? These questions seemed so important, but they frightened him, too. What if he never knew? What if Carissa resented him even asking? He knew he had no right to ask.

He focused on Odelia and Kent. Their love for each other made him smile. His parents seemed to find them ridiculous. He found them wonderful. As a boy, he'd always thought Odelia was a little odd, but he realized now that eccentricity was not the same as insufficiency. She was, perhaps, the wisest of them all. She certainly enjoyed life the most! He decided, secretly, that she was his favorite auntie. Not that he didn't love and value the others.

A feeling of such blessing swept over him that he almost laughed aloud. Fortunately, Tucker said something that made everyone chuckle, so no one noticed that Phillip might be unduly amused or pleased. It wouldn't have mattered if they had. He was too grateful to care at the moment, too determined, for he suddenly knew what he had to do, what he was supposed to do.

He'd never tried his hand at being a businessman; he'd never even thought of it until now, but somehow he knew that he had to at least make the attempt. A part of him acknowledged a certain fear or at least that he ought to be afraid of failure, but a larger part of him knew instinctively that this was what he'd been waiting all these weeks for, that this was the next big thing.

Oh, it wasn't like all the other times. The element of physical danger was missing, but nothing he had ever done had ever truly been important. This had meaning. So much meaning that he dared not even stop to think too much about it. But everything he'd done to this point just might have prepared him for this moment. He hoped and prayed that it was so, because he was about to take the biggest leap of faith of his life.

# *Chapter Thirteen*

After the meal, Phillip pitched in to straighten up the dining room and stow the few leftovers. Carissa sent the kids upstairs with instructions to change their clothes then quickly helped clean up before setting out after them. Phillip ran to catch up with her, ignoring the knowing looks that passed between Odelia and Kent.

"Carissa."

She stopped and half turned to face him. "Yes?"

"Do you think you might have some time for me a little later today? I mean, if you don't have plans."

"I don't have plans. Just give me time to change and get the kids settled."

He decided that if he was going to do this thing, he ought to do it right. His mind awhirl with plans, he asked, "Will a couple hours be okay with you?"

"Uh, sure."

A to-do list had been taking shape in his mind throughout the meal. It was a lot to get done in a short amount of time, but he thought he could pull it together if he had help. "I have to speak to my aunts. I'll see you later."

"Okay."

He didn't have time to explain more fully. Besides, it would be better to show her what he had in mind. Thankfully, his aunts were only too happy to help with his project. They understood that he and Carissa would need space to work that was close to the children, and Odelia had the perfect solution; the large storage room under the attic stairs beside Phillip's room would make a suitable office. It was on the same end of the house as the master suite and would be large enough for a desk, whiteboard and a couple of chairs. In addition, the attic contained enough space to set up a computer lab, as well as a play space for the children, if needed. Odelia asked Kent to help Phillip with the heavy work. She and Hypatia would figure out where to put everything unnecessary. Meanwhile, Magnolia volunteered to cull the attic for appropriate furnishings. While he changed his clothes, Phillip spared a few minutes to make a couple of phone calls. The first went to his brother. Then he got to work.

By the time he tapped on the door to the master suite, things were in place as much as possible. Carissa greeted him with a smile. Grace abandoned her TV show to try to climb Phillip, while Tucker rolled across the floor pretending to be a wrecking ball, and Nathan ignored him to read a book about boy archaeologists. Carissa invited Phillip to take a seat, but he'd barely sat down before Odelia and Kent arrived.

"I have something to show you," he explained to Carissa, passing Grace to Odelia. Nathan glared at him over the top of his book from the easy chair. "It won't take long," Phillip promised.

"Go see. Go see," Kent directed, waving them toward the door. "The missus and I will stay here with the children until you return."

Eager to show her, Phillip caught Carissa's hand and hauled her out of the suite.

"It's just an overlarge closet," he warned, dragging her along. "It doesn't even have a window, but there's room enough for a desk, a whiteboard and your laptop. Most importantly, it's private and quiet."

When he reached the former storage chamber, he threw open the door and stepped to one side. She put her head in and looked around.

"An office?"

"You can work here in peace," he told her. "The cordless phone reception is just fine. We've already checked. I'll watch the kids." She opened her mouth to speak, but he held up a hand. "Hear me out. I'm hoping that way you'll have time to work on the app. Now, come see this." He grabbed her hand again and hauled her to the foot of the attic stairs, then he went ahead of her, explaining. "I've spoken to my brother, and he's agreed to draw up formal partnership papers."

"Partnership, as in a business partnership."

"Exactly."

She seemed uncertain, so Phillip said, "I told him the split should be fifty-fifty, but if the terms aren't satisfactory, I'm open to negotiation. I know I can't do this without you, no matter how many contacts I have in the industry."

"No, that's fine," she said quickly, but then she fell silent as Phillip opened the attic door. "The kids will love it up here, but we're going to need equipment."

"Just give me a list," Phillip told her. "We have some underwriting, and I still have a few thousand in cash. Plus, my brother's offered to invest, too."

She gave him a surprised smile. "All right, but I can't promise how many hours I'll be able to dedicate to this project. I'll have to make a minimum number of sales every day before I can leave my regular job and go to work on the app. Agreed?"

"Absolutely. Do you think you could give me a few minutes now to estimate the cost of development? And I'll be wanting that equipment list as soon as possible, too. I've promised a business prospectus to a couple of people."

She raised her eyebrows at that but got down to business without delay. Phillip's excitement grew exponentially.

"Business partners," she said wryly. "Who'd have thought it?"

He clasped his hands behind him to keep from reaching out for her. This was business. For now. "Stranger things have happened, I suppose."

"Not that I can think of."

"Well, you know what they say about God working in mysterious ways."

"I think this definitely falls into that category," she agreed. "Now, I think it's time we rescue your aunt and uncle."

He chuckled at that. "You're probably right."

They returned to the master suite to find Nathan reading aloud to everyone. He was very good, his voice full of drama as he finished the tale of the boy archaeologist and a fearsome mummy.

Everyone applauded, including Phillip. Nathan couldn't hide a grin, even while he tried to give Phillip a dirty look. Perhaps that was why Phillip invited Carissa and her children out to dinner; he didn't feel like eating alone—or he didn't feel like letting Carissa out of his sight just yet. Strangest of all, he found that he wanted to spend some time with the children, too. Now, if he could just get through dinner without doing or saying something that would ruin the progress he'd made…

But everything seemed designed to try his patience. Grace almost spilled his iced tea. He had to track down Tucker and haul him back to the table three separate times, and Nathan vacillated between moody silence and downright rudeness. Despite all that, they managed to demolish two pizzas and make numerous trips to the salad bar in just over two hours. Through it all Carissa kept her cool, and so did Phillip. What was the point in losing his temper? Kids would be kids.

"You'll think twice before inviting us out again, I bet," Carissa said at the end of the meal, after she'd prevented Grace from attempting to bus their table.

"Maybe next time it could be just two of us," Phillip quipped, thinking that he'd like to take her for a nice, quiet, childless dinner.

Nathan snorted at that, challenging, "Like you'd take *me* anywhere."

Phillip felt as if he'd been smacked in the back

of the head with a hammer. Of course. Of all the children, Nathan would long for one-on-one time of any sort with anyone. How he must miss it, and Phillip suddenly wanted to give it to him.

"Well, now, Nathan. Where would you like to go, just you and me?"

Nathan looked away, but Grace immediately started jumping up and down.

"Me first! Me first!"

"You?" Phillip laughed. "And just where would you like to go, Miss Grace?"

"Tea party," she announced, folding her arms.

"I beg your pardon?"

"Tea party," she insisted, poking him in the thigh. "Just you and me."

That was how he came to be sitting at a table in the sunroom the next day wearing a big straw hat and a string of beads when his brother came to deliver the partnership papers. Asher put his hand over his mouth, but the snickers escaped just the same.

Phillip glowered and sank down a little farther in his chair. "Laugh now. You'll be doing the same in a few years. Just wait until Marie Ella plans a tea party for you."

"You're right," Asher admitted, grinning, "but I never expected to see *you* at it."

"That makes two of us," Phillip grumbled,

tossing the hat to the table and yanking the beads off.

"Lunch is over," Grace announced with a sigh.

"It certainly is," Phillip said, getting to his feet. He said to Grace, "I have work to do now." Then he kissed her on the forehead. Hilda came into the room, wiping her hands on a towel. "Grace promised to help you clean up after our tea party. Call upstairs when you're done. I'll send Nathan down for her."

"Chester can walk her back upstairs," Hilda said.

"Good idea. Otherwise, I'll have to dig her out of Odelia's closet again."

With that, Phillip and Asher headed up to the master suite to discuss the partnership terms with Carissa. As they climbed the stairs, Asher asked, "So, are you going to marry her?"

Phillip didn't pretend to misunderstand, but it took him a while to come up with an answer. "I seem to be headed in that direction."

Asher laughed, but to Phillip it was not a laughing matter. In fact, it was terrifying, and it got scarier almost by the hour.

After Carissa had looked over the partnership agreement and signed it, Asher went on his way. Phillip presented her with sales projection numbers.

"They aren't very thorough because I don't know how much to sell advertising for."

"Couldn't that wait until after the initial offering?" Carissa asked. "Once we have a better idea how many people might be interested in downloading the app, we'd have a better idea about advertising rates, wouldn't we?"

Phillip rubbed his chin thoughtfully. "That's not a bad business model. We might want to do that with the other apps we develop."

"Are we going to develop other apps?" she asked in surprise.

"If this works out, why not? Asher has some ideas about legal applications, and we did tell Garrett we'd look into his idea about identifying plants."

"You mean it? But…I failed at business before."

"Doesn't mean you'll fail again," he pointed out.

She stared at him for a long moment before dropping onto the couch. "You sound like Tom."

Phillip felt a chill seeping into his veins. He carefully took a seat on the edge of the cushion next to her.

"You're like him in many ways, frankly. It's that rugged, he-man exterior, that try-anything-once attitude." She threw out a hand. "Oh, you're more handsome, more polished, but then, you're a Chatam. No doubt, you're a jack-of-all-trades, just as he was."

"Jack-of-all-trades, master of none," Phillip muttered. "I've roughed it in the Canadian Northwest for months. I'm a skydiver of expert status, which means I'm suitable for instructing tourists. I've surfed every great beach in the world. I've worked as a commercial fisherman. And let's not forget the mountain climbing. Along the way, I've earned three degrees, none of which I've ever really used. Currently I live with my three elderly aunts. Yeah, I'm a real prize."

"Commercial fishing," she exclaimed, sitting up straight. "Surfing. Skydiving. Zoos. The Canadian Northwest! Phillip, we're talking about reality apps here. Why wouldn't it work for those things, as well as mountain climbing?"

He shot to his feet. "That's brilliant. And your father said you didn't have a head for business."

"I don't." She snatched up the folder and shook it at him. "But you do. All I do is write code and maybe do some computer design."

"Then together we ought to be able to make this work," he told her, pulling her to her feet.

She grinned. "I think so, too."

Could they make *more than* business work between them? Phillip wondered, looking down into her face. Oh, how he hoped so! His gaze dropped to her lips just as something hit him in the back of the legs, knocking him against her.

"It's my turn!"

He looked down to find Tucker stepping up onto the coffee table. Phillip plucked him off it. "Your turn?"

"To go to dinner alone with you. Where are we going?"

Phillip looked at Carissa, who did her best not to smile, and mentally sighed. He should've known. If he did it for one, of course he'd have to do it for all. "What's your favorite food?"

"Tacos!"

"Mexican it is."

"When?"

"It'll be a surprise."

"Soon!" Tucker demanded.

"We'll see," Carissa told him, indicating that Phillip should put him down. Phillip set Tucker on his feet, and Carissa pointed him toward his bedroom. "Out."

He ran, because Tucker never walked, shouting, "Oh, boy! Phillip's taking me to a Mexican restaurant!"

Carissa folded her arms. "I'm afraid you won't have a moment's peace until you do it."

Phillip gave her a sheepish look. "Might as well be tomorrow. Wednesday is church, and Thursday is grief support group."

She nodded. “Tomorrow.”

He grinned. “Does that mean you’ll ride to support group with me on Thursday?”

She chuckled. “Why not?”

“And church Wednesday night?” She hesitated, so he pressed. “They have lots of activities for the kids on Wednesdays.”

“That might be good for them. But you’d better ride with us. And it’s only if I make my quota early enough.”

“You’ll make your quota,” he told her, pleased. “I just know it. How can you not, with me hanging out with the rug rats?”

Smiling, she nodded. He stood there searching for something else to say for several seconds before dropping the folder onto the table and turning for the door. She followed him and then, at the last moment, laid a hand on his shoulder. He spun to face her.

“Phillip, are we crazy to think this might actually work?”

“I don’t know,” he told her honestly. “All I know is that when I pray about it, I feel…elated, almost. I think it’s something we have to do, have to try.”

“You pray about it,” she said softly, a note of awe in her voice and a faraway look in her eye. “I don’t know if Tom ever did that. He was a believer, but I don’t know if he ever did that.”

She looked up suddenly, smiling, and her face seemed to glow. "I'm glad you pray about it. I will, too, from now on."

Phillip suddenly wanted to hold her close, to never let her go again. He wanted so much: to offer financial security to Carissa and the kids, for Carissa to love and want him, marriage, family, the whole ball of wax. It was too much to even hope for, let alone ask for. Instead, he mutely nodded, ran his hands down her arms, squeezed her hands in his and left before he made an utter fool of himself.

Tuesday was a difficult day. The kids seemed to bounce off the walls, so Tucker surprised Phillip when they went to dinner together that evening. He kept himself at the table at the Mexican restaurant, talking and eating a mile a minute, his legs swinging. He talked about everything from Nathan being too bossy and Grace being too giggly to his mom being pretty.

"Anyway, I think she's pretty."

"She is," Phillip agreed. "Very pretty."

"So why don't you marry her?"

"I just might," Phillip heard himself say, his heartbeat suddenly echoing in his ears.

"When?" Tucker demanded.

"I don't know," Phillip answered with a nonchalance he didn't feel, "and I said *might.* She'd have to agree, and we're a long way from that. Eat your dinner."

Tucker forked up a huge bite of beans and rice, then said with a full mouth, "Me and Grace want you to."

Phillip's chest seemed to expand. He fought the feeling, scooting his chair a little closer to the table. "But Nathan doesn't, does he?"

"I think he might."

Phillip was surprised by that. Not much he'd done or said had ever met with Nathan's approval, but Phillip couldn't help hoping. "What makes you think so?"

Tucker shrugged. "Things have been better since you been around."

"Ah," Phillip said, disappointed. He wanted to ask how things had been better, but he didn't dare. It was likely that all the better things that Tucker and Grace ascribed to him were nothing more than a result of them living at Chatam House. No doubt, Nathan knew it, too. Still, at least Carissa's children had thought of him as a potential mate for her.

Maybe, though, he was too much like her late husband. The idea haunted Phillip, so much so that he had almost convinced himself to ask her when he took Tucker home after their dinner. Carissa was so concerned about how Tucker had behaved during dinner, however, that Phillip found himself reassuring her instead.

"I threatened to tie him to the bed for a week if he so much as left the table tonight," she said, looking down into Tucker's upturned face.

Phillip chuckled. "He must have taken you at your word, then, because he didn't budge."

"You're not just saying that?"

"He stayed put," Phillip told her, ruffling Tucker's hair.

"I'm so glad." She bent down and touched her nose to Tucker's, saying, "There's hope for you yet, my boy."

"Mo-om."

A huff from the direction of the hallway brought Phillip's attention to Nathan, who stood with arms folded, regarding them all, frowning. Phillip put on a smile.

"So where would you like to go for dinner, Nathan?"

"Nowhere."

"Nathan," Carissa said warningly.

He rolled his eyes. Phillip tamped down a spurt of irritation mixed with alarm.

"Aw, come on," he said, "what's your favorite food?"

"Nothing you'd like."

"Nathan, that's uncalled for," Carissa warned softly.

The boy sighed then muttered the name of an

expensive seafood restaurant that advertised on TV frequently.

Carissa smiled apologetically. "Nathan thinks he likes fish."

"I do!"

"But the other two aren't too keen on it," Carissa went on. "In truth, they haven't had much opportunity to eat fish, but Nathan used to eat it occasionally with his dad."

"He was a *great* fisherman, and we used to eat what he caught," Nathan insisted.

"He did like a mess of fried catfish," Carissa said quietly.

"Well, if it's catfish you like, Nathan, there's a great catfish restaurant here in town," Phillip ventured. "How does that sound?"

"Humph," Nathan said, and turning his back, he disappeared down the hallway.

He had to do this. He had to try. "How is Friday?"

"I can't imagine why you'd want to do this. You see how he behaves."

"Has any man spent time with Nathan alone since his dad died?" Phillip asked. She shook her head, shamefaced. "Seems to me that it can't hurt, then."

She smiled, and they agreed on Friday. Wisely, they agreed not to mention it again to Nathan until Phillip showed up to take him to dinner.

Meanwhile, he had the midweek service and the grief support meeting to look forward to.

Who would ever have dreamed that he'd actually look forward to grief support meetings?

## *Chapter Fourteen*

They went to midweek service the next evening at Downtown Bible Church in Carissa's old van. She had made her sales quota early, but the day had not been without calamity. Tucker and Nathan got into a fistfight while Phillip was chatting on the phone with an old surfing buddy. Grace wandered off to play in Odelia's closet again, but at least Phillip knew to look for her there first. All in all, however, Carissa was pleased. Phillip had proved surprisingly laid-back with the children, and despite her personal disappointment where Phillip was concerned, Carissa somehow felt that she could stop holding her breath.

The prayer meeting calmed her nerves even more. What was happening between her and Phillip Chatam might be nothing more than business and casual friendship, but she felt sure that it would ultimately play out to her benefit. She constantly prayed for God to temper her expectations so that she would be open to His will rather than caught up in her own wishes. That way, she feared, lay disappointment and bitterness when she wanted to be open only to obedience and gratitude.

Thursday went so smoothly that she felt a little weird. Phillip showed up during breakfast, which had become the normal routine of the day, and suggested that he and the children would swim in the afternoon *if* they allowed him to make a few phone calls uninterrupted during the morning. They promised to cooperate and then made good on their promises. Even more surprising, Carissa made more than her quota of sales by midafternoon and was able to get up to the computer lab, now fully stocked with equipment, before evening.

While the children played quietly, subdued by their romp in the pool earlier, Carissa and Phillip worked on the initial design of the app. She'd been toying with it, and Phillip's experiences with mountain climbing helped her refine the look and feel of it.

Dallas arrived that evening, joining Phillip and the aunties for dinner, then went up to the master suite to stay with the children while Phillip and Carissa attended the grief support meeting.

When they arrived, they found that a new couple had joined the group.

Middle-aged and fit, the Tillotsons were both doctors whose handicapped son had died of natural causes. They had thought themselves well prepared, but his death had taken them by surprise, nonetheless. As everyone shared their stories and encouraged them, Carissa realized that her own grief and fear had truly lessened, thanks to the warmth and support she had experienced from the group.

As the meeting broke, Mrs. Tillotson shocked Carissa when she commented, "I've heard that many couples find each other in grief counseling." Her gaze swung back and forth between Carissa and Phillip. "I suppose it's as good a way to meet as any."

Carissa blinked. Phillip, meanwhile, reached across and shook hands with the lady's husband before turning to his uncle, acting as if he hadn't heard the comment. Suddenly, Carissa felt as if she skated on the edge of disappointment, heartbreak a yawning chasm beneath her. She'd told herself over and over that she wouldn't expect more than a business partnership from Phillip, but she'd been fooling herself all along. She wanted more from him. Hoping for anything else was just asking for trouble. So why, oh, why couldn't she stop?

* * *

On Friday evening, Nathan acted as if he was going to a hanging. He dragged his feet and moped, but he accompanied Phillip to his car, got in and allowed himself to be driven to the restaurant, which was located in a picturesque turn-of-the-century house near the Buffalo Creek downtown square. The menu ranged from fried catfish to fried pickles with fried sweet potatoes and fried cheese thrown in to balance things. Nathan didn't like anything except the fish, and he was iffy about that at first. His usual surliness remained unimproved by the experience.

After a while, he asked Phillip, "Why're you doing this?"

Phillip shrugged. "Seemed like a good idea at the time. Besides, I like catfish."

"You like my mom more," Nathan accused.

Phillip just nodded. "I like you, too," he said.

"Well, I *don't* like you," Nathan grumbled, "and making me eat fish with you isn't going to change that."

"What will change it?" Phillip asked.

"Nothing," Nathan snapped, "because you aren't my dad and you never will be."

"Nathan, I'm not trying to be your dad," Phillip said. Unfortunately, he knew the words were a lie the instant they left his mouth. What was he doing if not trying to befriend Carissa's children? Wasn't he trying to prove to himself that he could be good father and husband material?

"I just want my real dad," Nathan muttered.

They were an awful lot alike, he and Nathan, both wanting something they couldn't have. Nathan wanted his dad back. Phillip wanted to be a different kind of man. The kind who might actually have something to offer this boy and his mother, something more substantial than an occasional dinner out. He didn't even have his own place to live or a regular paycheck. Shouldn't he be able to do anything, for the possibility of making a life with Carissa and her children?

*Lord, make me what they need,* he prayed. *Or give me the strength to get out of the way so they can have it with someone else.*

They returned to the house in silence. Nathan stared out the window of the car, saying nothing. Phillip let the boy be. His own inadequacies weighed on him like a mountain of rock. He couldn't help remembering the stunned look on Carissa's face the evening before, when Mrs. Tillotson had so casually assumed that they were a couple. It was as if the thought had never occurred to Carissa before that moment. Phillip had felt as if she'd stabbed a hatpin into his forehead, for he had thought of little else since he'd first met her.

Carissa opened the door to the suite before

they could even knock, her anxiety obvious. Nathan put her out of her misery, drawling sarcastically, "I told you I liked fish."

She looked to Phillip. "He ate it, then?"

"A whole platter."

Nathan gazed up at Phillip then headed toward his bedroom. Carissa called him back with a sharp "Nathan!"

The boy stopped and looked back over his shoulder. Phillip spared him the effort of saying thanks.

"You're welcome."

Nathan shrugged and went on his way. Phillip felt like all his hopes were disappearing with him. He had to accept that all he would ever have with Carissa Hopper was a business partnership. He prayed fervently that it would turn into something to give Carissa and her kids a bit of financial security. Then he was going to leave, go far away from Chatam House and Buffalo Creek. Meanwhile, he would put his nose to the grindstone.

Over the next week, Phillip picked up fairly quickly on what Carissa was doing—not the code, but the design part of the work. She had an orderly mind but also a cool aesthetic sense when it came to the placement of widgets and buttons and other design elements. He contributed by culling an amazing photo from his own reel, which he then digitized, for use as their icon. She was thrilled with the result and hugged him. The gesture seemed perfectly natural—until they looked up and found all three of the children staring at them. Grace and Tucker grinned at each other, but Nathan stomped off in a huff.

Carissa put a hand to her hair self-consciously. Phillip took a deep, silent breath, suddenly aware that their every gesture was being scrutinized. He didn't realize how much until a throat cleared behind them. Carissa and he whirled around to find his parents standing at the head of the attic stairs. Dallas was with them.

His father waved a patrician hand. "So these are the offices of Chopper Apps, LLC, I presume."

They had chosen the name Chopper as an amalgam of Chatam and Hopper. It had seemed clever at the time. The way Murdock said it, the name sounded cheesy. Dallas sent Carissa an apologetic glance, even as Maryanne Chatam walked across the floor to stoop before Grace.

"Hello," she said. "I'm Phillip's mother."

Grace's eyes grew as round as saucers. Then she put her hands on her knees and started to laugh, pointing at Maryanne.

Maryanne gaped at Phillip, but he didn't have an explanation.

At the same time, Tucker zipped over to Murdock, asking, "You his father?"

"I am..." Murdock cleared his throat. "...Phillip's father. And also Dallas's father."

"Bffn!" Grace called gleefully, waving at Dallas, who sent her a tiny wave back. Grace covered her mouth with her hand, still laughing at Maryanne.

One look at Carissa's glowing pink face had Phillip on his feet. He walked over and plucked Grace up off the floor. "Just what's so funny, funny face?"

"Your mommy looks like a grandma," she said.

Maryanne pushed up to her feet, chucked Grace under the chin and said, "I *am* a grandma, young lady, and proud of it. My granddaughter isn't nearly as big as you, but I think you'd like her, because she's adorable."

"*I'm* adorable," Grace said confidently, and Carissa gasped, but Phillip had to smile.

"Don't you have a grandmother?" Maryanne asked.

Grace considered this, sighed and said, "I just have a Lexi."

Before his mother could ask what a "Lexi" was, Phillip set Grace on her feet and gave her a little shove. "Why don't you go downstairs with your mom so I can show my parents around?"

Carissa snapped her fingers, and for once the children responded just as they should, allowing themselves to be herded down the stairs easily. Phillip prepared to be grilled, toasted and roasted.

To his surprise, Dallas lifted a hand and said, "Before this goes one step further, I just want it on the record that Asher is the one who called them."

Phillip decided he needed to have a long discussion with his brother, but after spending the afternoon with his parents, he decided that he just might have to thank his big brother.

Murdock and Maryanne were waiting when Carissa returned from church with the children the next day. They sat on the front porch of Chatam House in their Sunday best with a low wrought iron table between them. Phillip stood at the top of the stairs, leaning against one of the thick, white columns, while Dallas swayed idly in the porch swing. Carissa had seen nothing of Phillip or his parents after their unexpected visit to the attic computer lab the day before. She didn't know if that was good or bad, but she feared the worst.

Gulping, she brushed lint from the skirt of her navy blue suit after stepping out from behind the steering wheel of her old van. Hilda and

Chester had taken their own car so they could join friends from their Sunday-school class for a potluck luncheon. Before Carissa could instruct them otherwise, the children spilled out of the van on their own, Tucker first, as usual, then Nathan. His gaze darted warily behind his glasses as he helped Grace from her safety seat. Walking around the front end of the vehicle, Carissa knew just how he felt.

Phillip started down the steps as she and the children moved up the walk. Grace skipped toward him, but Carissa snagged her hand, holding her back. He smiled down at the girl before lifting his gaze to Carissa's face.

"My parents and I would like to take you to lunch. To, um, discuss business." He glanced around, adding quickly, "Dallas and the aunties will watch over the children, if that's all right."

Heart pounding, Carissa thought, *This is it, then.* She felt sure that his parents had convinced him to drop their partnership. Well, it was for the best. The business was likely destined for failure anyway.

Phillip beckoned to Dallas, saying, "We'd better go. Every church in town will have let out by now. We'll be lucky to get a table in less than an hour."

"We'll get a table," Murdock said, appearing at his shoulder. "It's all arranged." Maryanne stepped up to his side. He took her by the elbow and walked her past Carissa out onto the graveled drive, where a luxury sedan sat.

Carissa looked up at Phillip, took a deep breath and let him lead her toward the car.

Murdock drove straight to the finest Italian restaurant in town, and the proprietor met him at the hostess desk. They were shown to a table in a private room at once. After the drinks were brought and the orders were taken, Phillip sat back in his chair and began to speak.

"Mom and Dad want to invest in our company."

Carissa's heart stopped. Were they offering to buy her out?

"What do you think?" he asked. "I told them I couldn't accept without consulting you."

"It would just be a matter of operating capital," Murdock explained. "Enough so you could open a real office."

"Or move out on your own," Maryanne said, with a shake of her head and a droll smile, as if she and Carissa had a secret. "Men are always putting the cart before the horse."

"I'm not sure I understand."

"It's not just that we're glad to have him off that mountain," Murdock rumbled. "This thing really seems to have potential, and Phillip is totally convinced you can pull it off."

"If anyone can, Carissa can," Phillip said, smiling at her.

"Some operating capital would mean that you wouldn't have to work the other job," Maryanne put in meaningfully.

"That decision is Carissa's," Phillip pointed out. "You were a working mother. You would know how that is."

"Let's be honest," Maryanne said bluntly, meeting Carissa's gaze. "I was more than a working mother. I was a career woman with children, and I didn't always get the balance right. It's tough enough when you have a husband and multiple resources at your fingertips. I can't imagine how you manage on your own."

Stunned, Carissa floundered for a moment before admitting, "Not always well."

Maryanne looked at Phillip, smiling. "Hopefully, that will change for the better."

Phillip reached across the table and covered Carissa's hand with his. "What do you say, partner? Ready to take on a couple of investors and grab the future by the horns?"

Several seconds passed before reality set in. They weren't offering to buy her out. They were offering to pour money into Chopper Apps, enough so that she wouldn't have to sell computer services over the telephone if she didn't want to! She wasn't sure what to say or do, especially about giving up her job. That seemed like an awfully big step to take, but with the Chatams behind this new project, her hopes soared.

Without realizing that she'd turned her palm up to meet Phillip's, she closed her eyes and said a quick prayer of thanks before nodding her head.

"Sounds great. It sounds just great."

Phillip's fingers threaded through hers and squeezed. She couldn't stop her huge smile or the fluttering of her heart.

It didn't seem possible. Phillip could barely grasp the concept. Not only did his parents approve of the business venture, they hadn't said one word, negative or otherwise, about a romantic involvement between him and Carissa. In fact, they gave it their tacit approval in a very shocking way. After dinner on Sunday, they spent the remainder of the day with Asher, Ellie and Marie Ella. As requested, Phillip and Dallas put in an appearance at the evening meal, during which Maryanne casually suggested that she and Murdock take Carissa's children on an outing the next day, Monday, so he and Carissa could concentrate on business. Dumbfounded, Phillip must have stared at her for fifteen full seconds, after which she put down her fork and calmly reminded him that she was a pediatrician who had raised four children of her own.

"I think I'm fully capable of handling three precocious youngsters."

Dallas promptly volunteered to go along.

Phillip managed to stammer, "I'll r-run the idea by Carissa t-tonight and get back to you."

Carissa, of course, could not realize how unlike his parents the idea was. She assumed they were so anxious to see a return on their investment that they'd even babysit her children so she could work on the project. "I guess I could skip making calls tomorrow, and the kids would certainly enjoy the outing."

Phillip let her think what she liked, but even the aunties stood at the door of Chatam House with their jaws ajar as Grace, Tucker and a very disgruntled Nathan trailed out between Murdock and Maryanne the next morning, a worried-looking Dallas bringing up the rear. Their destination was the Dallas aquarium. Personally, Phillip thought they'd get halfway through the place, lose Tucker, spend the rest of the afternoon searching for him and return home in a sullen huff. He stopped worrying about his parents and the children when, after hours of feverish work and several disappointments, the initial phase of the app finally performed like a charm.

Phillip had done nothing more than what he'd been told. Carissa was the boss in the lab, and he couldn't have been more proud. Elated, he scooped Carissa up out of her chair and swung her around the room.

"I knew it! I knew it. You're a genius."

He plopped her down again, aiming an impulsive kiss at her cheek. Laughing, she unexpectedly turned her head just enough to bring her lips into contact with his.

They both froze as electricity zapped through the air. Then Phillip slowly straightened. Carissa turned back to the computer terminal, her fingers flying across the keyboard. He let his hand lightly caress the back of her head.

"Call Seattle," she said, her voice sounding strangled. "Have them turn on the camera. We're ready for transmission."

Phillip fought with himself, torn between hauling her up out of that chair to kiss her and doing as she asked. In the end, he put the business ahead of his personal needs. This was the ticket to financial independence for her and the children, their chance at the kind of life they needed and deserved. He called Seattle.

Nearly two hours of frustration later, they finally got a clear picture transmitting through Phillip's smartphone. By the time they were done, Carissa had worked all the bugs out and secured the uplink. Before they broke the connection, Phillip learned that one of the guides was taking up a party of six in two days. They expected at least three to reach the summit and one or more to cross the crater at the top of Mount Rainier and sign the book kept in the metal box there. It would be a climb worth transmitting and filming.

"Our first live transmission, and the first for our archive," Carissa stated.

The climb could be viewed in real time, or the film could be watched later. They posted the app to go live thirty minutes after the start of the climb. In two days, they would be in business. While the transmission would run, uninterrupted on their live feed, they agreed not to track how many people were downloading the app until after church on Wednesday night.

His parents returned the children that evening with barely a word about how the day had gone. Nathan seemed more subdued than usual, but then, all of the children were obviously tired. Grace babbled about the penguins, Tucker mentioned the eels, and all three clutched pricey gifts that Phillip's parents had bought them. For Nathan, it was a large, glossy book about the oceans. Tucker got a model of a shark with a working jaw, and Grace carried a stuffed walrus almost as big as her. Phillip looked at Dallas, trying to ratchet his jaw back into place, but she just shrugged and offered him a limp smile.

Were these the same people who had considered Ellie too young and eccentric for Asher and had urged Petra to focus on career rather than marriage, until a mere carpenter had come calling? Nevertheless, Phillip couldn't imagine that becoming grandparents had softened his parents so much that they were not just willing but eager to accept a penniless widow and three less-than-perfect children into the family. Perhaps they thought that once Carissa was financially sound and independent, she would have no more use for their vagabond younger son.

When Carissa started to protest that his parents shouldn't have spent so much money, Phillip interrupted to announce that the app would go live on Wednesday morning. Murdock and Maryanne greeted this news enthusiastically. Then Murdock confirmed Phillip's worst suspicions by clapping a hand onto Dallas's shoulder and saying, "Call that Realtor friend of yours, honey. I think Chopper Apps needs a new home!"

Carissa said that she needed to work, but Maryanne waved that away, saying that Carissa shouldn't let Phillip and his father make all the decisions.

"You'll wind up working in luxury offices and living in Chatam House from now on, if you do. Of course, if you want to stay on in Chatam House..."

"No," Carissa hastily retorted. "No, we've imposed long enough."

"It's no imposition," Phillip assured her firmly.

"Dallas, you'll stay with the children, won't you?" Maryanne asked smoothly.

Dallas shuttled a glance helplessly back and forth between Phillip and their mother. "Of course, if that's what everyone wants."

"Well, it's settled, then," Murdock decreed heartily. "We'll go right after breakfast tomorrow."

Phillip glanced at Carissa, ready to argue the matter if she balked, but she nodded. His parents took their leave of the children with handshakes and shoulder pats, but at the very end, Phillip caught a wink that his father sent Nathan. The boy's conspiratorial smile turned the butterflies in Phillip's stomach to lead weights.

Something was afoot. Phillip just knew it, and he meant to find out what it was.

# *Chapter Fifteen*

After his parents and Dallas left, Phillip hung around the suite while Carissa spoke to the children about their day. Dr. Maryanne, as they'd been told to call Phillip's mother, had apparently anticipated Tucker's every move and kept him smoothly in check, leaving Grace to her "bffn" Dallas and Doc to shepherd Nathan. He could just imagine his father pumping Nathan for information about his mother's relationship with Phillip.

Because the children were tired, Phillip stuck around to help tuck them into bed. He was shocked when Nathan sat up in the lower bunk and said, "Doc doesn't treat me like a stupid little kid."

Phillip glanced into the hallway, saw Carissa pass into the sitting room and backed up, carefully closing the door behind him. He crouched down beside the bed. "That's because you're not a stupid little kid."

Nathan flopped down onto the pillow and folded his arms atop the covers. "Doc says the Chatams don't have stupid kids."

"He's right about that."

"But I'm not a Chatam."

Phillip wanted to say that he could be. Instead, he said, "So, what else did you two talk about?"

Nathan removed his glasses and set them on the bedside table before softly answering, "Forgiveness."

Jolted, Phillip sat cross-legged on the floor. "What about forgiveness?"

Nathan drew his brows together. "Doc says I'm mad at God for letting my dad die."

Phillip caught his breath, but he managed to keep his cool.

Nathan continued. "Doc said I could just ask God to forgive me, and He would, because of everything Jesus did on the cross."

"That's right," Phillip managed.

Nathan went on in a thick voice. "Doc said I could say it anywhere, anytime, that I didn't have to wait for church or anything. So I prayed with him."

Phillip reached out and clasped the boy's hand. "You know something, Nathan? I need to ask for forgiveness, too. I haven't always given my dad the respect and honor he's due. Maybe…maybe you could help me pray now."

Nathan rolled onto his side, facing Phillip, and closed his eyes. "Sure," he said, his hand still in Phillip's. "Just say, 'God, I'm sorry' and stuff."

Smiling, Phillip began to pray, words pouring out of him without thought. "Lord, thank You for my father, and thank You for Nathan's father. I don't know why Nathan didn't get to keep his, but I'm glad I got to keep mine, and I'm glad I get to know Nathan. Forgive me for not always appreciating my dad and how much he cares for me. Forgive me for not always appreciating You and how much You care for me and all of Your children. Help me make my dad proud. And Nathan, too. And You especially. In Jesus's name. Amen."

"Amen," Nathan said.

"Amen" came from the top bunk.

Nathan rolled his eyes. Phillip bit his lip and winked. Nathan rolled onto his back and showed every sign of falling asleep. Phillip resisted the urge to ruffle his hair and instead rose to swiftly cross the room and slip out.

He took a moment to compose himself before sauntering into the sitting room. Carissa looked up from the sofa. "Everything okay?"

"Sure. Nathan just wanted to talk for a minute."

"Oh?"

"Yeah, he likes my dad," Phillip said lightly. "Go figure."

Her brow furrowed as if she wasn't quite sure what to make of that, but then she smiled. "Sounds like they had quite a day."

"Mmm-hmm."

"Well," she said, abruptly getting to her feet, "we have a busy day scheduled tomorrow. Best call it a night."

He let her see him out, knowing that he had some thinking and praying—and maybe some growing up—to do. He'd jumped from experience to experience, relishing the new and the unusual, responsible for no one and nothing but himself. He'd felt himself beneath the attention of God, and that had been fine with him—until he'd met Carissa and her children. Now he knew how wrong he'd been. God had been trying to get his attention for a very long time, and he had ignored Him, just as he'd ignored his parents.

Phillip had never worried about finding or keeping a job, always knowing that he could find work somehow doing something, but now he was afraid to fail and afraid to succeed. If he failed, Carissa and her children would continue to suffer, and if he succeeded… The idea that Carissa and the kids might not need him anymore was almost more than he could bear. He loved them. He loved her. He loved everything about her:

her never-say-die determination, her work ethic, her pragmatism, the dreaminess in her deep blue eyes that she tried so hard to hide, her laughter and her tears, her breathtaking beauty and the way she fit into his arms. He even loved the way she accepted each of her children for the individuals they were and how she revered her late husband's memory, though he had left her in a heap of trouble.

For the first time in his life, Phillip Chatam had found something that he truly wanted, and he had no idea how to get it. All he could do was ask God to make him worthy of Carissa and her children. He wished fervently that he'd listened to his parents when they'd counseled him to build for the future—and prayed that it wasn't too late.

Nathan's cheerfulness worried Carissa. She feared that he knew Phillip's parents intended to torpedo his relationship with her, with Nathan's help, no doubt. Still, it was all in God's hands. She couldn't make Phillip want her—them—and she couldn't make his parents approve. All she could do was trust God to do what was best for her and the kids. So she rose Tuesday morning and prepared herself to spend the day viewing office space with Phillip and his parents. When she called her employer to say that she would be taking off another day, she was warned that her job was in jeopardy. She had done well the previous week, but if she failed to meet her monthly quota, she would be fired. So be it.

Immediately after breakfast, they set out, with Phillip driving his father's car and Murdock sitting beside him, leaving Carissa in the backseat with Maryanne. They looked at a number of properties: one particularly attractive office building just off the downtown square, several unique structures with many commercial possibilities and what amounted to an estate with a large house and a barn converted to a small leather-goods factory that had outgrown its space. The final stop was a spacious but affordable home in a well-established neighborhood a couple of blocks off Main Street. Zoned as mixed use, the house occupied a large lot with deep driveways on both sides. One led to a three-car garage, the other to an attached office of a similar size. It was the house itself that captivated Carissa, however.

Built of creamy brick and native rock with a tan roof, it might have appeared rather vanilla in appearance if not for the graceful crepe myrtles, sheltering oak trees, neat shrubbery and clinging ivy that surrounded the building. She knew that the children would flip over the pool in the backyard, a smaller version of the one at Chatam House, but Carissa stared in delight at the pale tile floors that flowed through the light, airy great room and the large, open kitchen, separated only by a freestanding fireplace with a deep hearth all the way around. Four bedrooms and a den completed the first floor with a game room above. This was the kind of home where children could run and play as they grew, where a couple could entertain friends poolside on a summer day or fireside during the winter.

"This would be perfect for you and the children," Phillip said, "and the office space seems adequate."

"But what about you?" Carissa asked.

"Oh, he can stay on at Chatam House," Maryanne put in nonchalantly.

"For now," Murdock added.

Ignoring his parents, Phillip took her hand in his. "You really like this place, don't you?"

She chose not to answer that. It would be unfair for her to wind up with this beautiful home while all Phillip got out of it was a place to work. "I think we need to pray about it."

Maryanne looked around with dismay on her face. "Oh, but it's such a perfect—"

Her husband cleared his throat, his hands alighting upon her shoulders. "Carissa has a point. It never hurts to say an extra prayer on a matter."

"You're right, Dad," Phillip said.

Murdock harrumphed, cleared his throat again and gave his wife a nudge, saying, "Let's give these two a moment to talk, shall we?" Maryanne nodded, and they went out.

"We'll pray on it," Phillip said, watching his parents through the window as they got into the car, Maryanne in the front passenger seat this time, "but something tells me this is the place."

The place for her and her children, Carissa thought. Then he would be free to carry on with his adventures. Without them. She looked around at this beautiful house and her eyes swelled with tears.

After checking to make sure that the app had gone live as planned, Carissa insisted on working at her regular job on Wednesday. Phillip insisted on taking care of the children so she could make phone calls. His parents insisted on staying in town one more day.

"You agreed not to track participation until this evening after church," Murdock said at breakfast. "So, we'll get the first reading on the success of this thing, then we'll be on our way in the morning."

Phillip seemed not to mind, and Carissa couldn't see what difference it made. Phillip would do what Phillip would do, no matter what his parents wanted. He always had. He interrupted her just after lunch to say that the head of advertising of a climbing-gear manufacturer had called him to inquire about buying ad space with Chopper Apps. Phillip had promised to put the company's name on a list and get back to them.

"That's a good sign, don't you think?"

"A very good sign."

Nevertheless, by the time they left for the midweek service, Carissa felt that her insides were tied into knots. She prayed fervently for the success of the business, the well-being of each of her children and for Phillip. She prayed for herself, too.

Phillip drove her old van as they returned home after church. As they crested the slight rise in the long, circular drive, a trio of vehicles came into view: the aunties' town car, his parents' sedan and one other. Carissa groaned.

At the same time, Grace cried, "Lexi!"

"Oh, no," Phillip and Nathan said in unison.

"Just what we need," Carissa muttered.

"It'll be okay," Phillip promised, but the idea of his parents and her mother in the same room was enough to make Carissa physically ill.

They found them sizing up one another in the front parlor. The aunties had already made the introductions and ordered a tea tray. Alexandra seemed to be trying to decide how to enlist these newest Chatams to her cause.

"Both doctors," she purred from the settee next to Magnolia. "Impressive. Then again, the Chatams have so many more resources than most folks. I guess that's why my daughter has taken such shameful advantage of your sisters, Dr. Chatam, sir." Behind her, Leander shifted uncertainly.

"No one takes advantage of my sisters, madam," Murdock said, taking a stern tone. "It is impossible to take advantage of those as generous as my older sisters."

"At any rate," Maryanne put in from a striped wing chair, "Carissa is almost family."

"Oh, my, yes," Hypatia agreed smoothly from her usual seat. "Why, she is the dearest niece of our own Chester."

"And our son's business partner," Murdock added, moving to stand behind Maryanne's chair, Dallas perching daintily upon the chair's arm.

Kent occupied another side chair. Odelia sat upon its twin next to him, her vibrant red-and-yellow-striped suit in stark contrast to the tasteful gold damask upholstery. Phillip, Carissa and the children clustered together in front of the fireplace, until Alexandra enticed Grace to come to her as Chester carried in the tea tray.

"Don't you want to sit in Lexi's lap, darling? I'll share my sweets with you."

Grace looked to her mother for permission

and, at Carissa's nod, slipped across the room. The aunties passed around cups of tea and plates of goodies. Chester hovered near the door, shadowed by Hilda.

"Now, what is this about a business?" Alexandra asked offhandedly as Grace nibbled cookies.

"Carissa has developed a smartphone app," Phillip explained succinctly.

Alexandra chuckled dismissively. "More of her computer nonsense. It never comes to anything."

"It will this time," Carissa said softly. "It was Phillip's idea, you see, and the Chatams have invested in it."

"You'll run it into the ground, Carissa," Alexandra predicted, "just as you did the last time."

"This is different," Carissa asserted.

"For one thing," Phillip said, "this is a viable thing. For another, she's not alone anymore."

"For how long?" Alexandra scoffed. "Until you run off to your next little adventure? I know all about you, Phillip Chatam. Before long, you'll be off flying helicopters or hang gliding or something else equally foolish."

"I won't," Phillip insisted, looking down at Carissa. His hand found hers and pressed it. "I promise you. We'll do this together."

"They're already doing it together," Maryanne observed, "and very well, it seems to me."

"Carissa is no more equipped than you to run a business," Alexandra said to Phillip, ignoring Maryanne. "She has three children, and because she refuses to let anyone help her, it'll be years before she's free to concentrate on anything else."

"You won't help me by splitting my family," Carissa said flatly.

"There. You see? She won't take help even when it's best for her little ones," Alexandra accused, wrapping her arms around Grace.

"You are *not* splitting up this family," Phillip declared with some heat. Carissa noticed that Nathan slid back a step and pressed close to Phillip's side. Tucker, who stood in front of his mother, tilted his head back to gaze up at Phillip.

"I don't see what you have to say about it," Alexandra sniffed.

"He might have a lot to say about it," Maryanne muttered. Carissa cut a sharp look at her, at which point she rolled her eyes. "Oh…just marry the woman, Phillip, and have done with it."

Phillip gaped at her. "But you…you said she'd targeted me!"

Maryanne waved that away. "I only wanted to see if you'd defend her, and you did. It's as plain as the nose on your face that you adore her." Carissa gasped. "Even your brother says it's just a matter of time before you marry, so do it."

Grace screamed with delight and jumped off Alexandra's lap. Running to Dallas, she threw up her arms, crying, "Auntie!"

Dallas caught her and swung her up. Glancing around guiltily, she explained, "I told her she couldn't call me that until…that is, unless…"

"No more bffn!" Grace declared, grinning.

"Best friends *for now,*" Carissa murmured.

"You haven't reformed at all!" Phillip blurted. "What on earth made you think…?"

"I don't know," Dallas all but wailed, half in apology, half in defense. "It's just that when I saw you with these three and then her, it seemed like a match. But all I ever did was tell them what a good guy you are."

"And that you need us," Tucker put in.

"As much as we need you," Nathan added in a rusty voice.

Carissa's mouth fell open. "Nathan?"

Suddenly Phillip squeezed her hand hard enough to break bones.

"I, um, don't know that I really have very much to offer, n-nothing that you and your mom don't already have," he said.

"Yes, you do," she said softly, urgently.

"Do I?" he asked, finally looking down at her.

"Oh, Phillip," she whispered, clasping his

hand with both of hers, "you've given me more hope than anyone ever has."

"Hope," he echoed. "It takes more than *hope,* sweetheart."

"I have hope because of the things you've done," she said, "everything from grief support to moving us in here, taking a hand with the kids, coming up with the app and inviting me to take part, even getting your family and friends to buy in. You've even made me feel pretty again."

"You aren't pretty," he told her. "You're beautiful. And I love you, Carissa. I love all of you."

She twisted, shook free of him and threw her arms around his neck. "I love you, too! I have for a long time. I didn't dare dream that you could feel the same way."

"Shhh." He folded her close. And felt Nathan's arms steal about his waist from behind. He reached down a hand to the boy, only to feel Tucker jumping up and down on his foot and Grace climbing him like a tree. Chuckling, he caught them all up in the sweep of one arm.

"Daddy Phil," Grace piped, "Doc Doc is crying."

"What?"

"Doc Doc is crying."

Phillip looked around to find his father with big tears rolling down his patrician cheeks.

"I am so proud of you, son," Murdock said in

a thick voice. "I daresay, Carissa and the children are the best thing that's ever happened to you, but you put your mind to making Chopper Apps a success for them, and you've done it."

"The app!" Phillip exclaimed, setting down the children and catching Carissa's hand. "I forgot."

He strode for the door, towing her with him. She threw a hopeful smile at the assembly, motioning for them to follow. Teacups rattled in saucers as everyone rose to join the parade. Up the stairs they went to the attic. Carissa brought the system online. A few keystrokes brought up a rolling ticker. Dallas gasped.

"Are those actual numbers of people who have downloaded the app and are viewing the climb?"

"This is unbelievable!" Carissa exclaimed.

Phillip put his hands to his head in shock. "Praise God!" he finally breathed. "It's beyond my wildest dreams."

"I knew it!" Murdock exclaimed, hugging Maryanne. "Call your brother and tell him."

Excitedly, Phillip pulled out his phone. He'd muted it during the church service and now found that he had numerous messages. As he began thumbing through them, Carissa rose from her chair.

"What is it?"

"They're all companies who want to buy

advertising," he said, stunned. "We've done it, babe. We've done it!"

Carissa lifted a hand to her trembling lips. "God did this," she whispered. "He made it all happen."

"Yes," Phillip agreed, hugging her. "Oh, yes. And I thought He didn't even notice."

"Are we billionaires?" Tucker asked excitedly.

Phillip laughed. "No, son, we're not, but we're considerably better off than we were. And tomorrow," he went on, gazing into Carissa's deep blue eyes, "I think we should go buy a certain house."

Maryanne clapped her hands. "It's a wonderful house," she promised the children.

"A wonderful house," Carissa agreed, tears standing in her eyes.

The aunties began talking excitedly about all the furniture up here that needed a good home, while Maryanne told the children about the house. Phillip noticed that Nathan went to stand beside Murdock and that his father's hand rested comfortably on the boy's shoulder.

Carissa looked around and asked, "Where is Alexandra?"

"The Hedgespeths slipped out the front door as we were headed upstairs," Dallas reported.

Carissa nodded knowingly. Phillip caught her hand. "Maybe she finally knows she's beaten."

"What she knows is that Carissa with a husband is much more formidable than Carissa without a husband," Dallas said, "especially if that husband is a Chatam."

Carissa smiled and wrapped her arms around Phillip's waist, while Odelia quoted from Scripture.

"'Two are better than one, because they have a good return for their labor: If either of them falls down, one can help the other up. But pity anyone who falls and has no one to help them up.'"

"No pity for me," Phillip said, looking deeply into Carissa's wondrous blue eyes.

"Or me," she replied happily.

So he kissed her, finally, there in front of God and everyone.

# *Epilogue*

Watching Phillip watch his wife of hours laugh and flit about the room in a formfitting dress of knee-length pale peach accompanied by a matching swirl of organza veil that reached her slender waist, Odelia Chatam couldn't help smiling. He had ditched his suit coat and loosened his tie as soon as he'd come in the door, rolling his shirtsleeves to his elbows. Then he and Carissa had spent the next half hour welcoming wedding guests into their home, while his sisters and his mother had hurried to lay out Hilda's buffet. It was a most unusual wedding reception, but quite enjoyable. Then again, it had been a most unusual wedding.

The bride had been escorted down the aisle by both of her sons. Her daughter had served as the flower girl, and the groom's parents had stood up with the happy couple as best man and matron of honor.

Smiling happily, Phillip carried a canned soft drink over to the living-room window seat and folded himself down beside her, giving her that you're-my-favorite-aunt smile of his. Oh, yes, she knew it well and treasured the knowledge. She saw no harm in it. The aunties all had their favorites among their nieces and nephews. It didn't mean that they loved the others any less.

"You don't mind that we did it here instead of Chatam House, do you?" he asked softly.

"Not a bit," she told him, patting his hand. "Now, Hypatia may be another story. You know what stock she sets on big, formal wedding receptions."

Phillip grinned and tweaked the pouf on her pink pillbox hat. "Hypatia did a swell job on your wedding and reception, as I recall."

Odelia clasped her hands together, feeling the pink poufs of her earrings sway at the ends of their chains. "Didn't she, though?"

His laughter boomed across the room, and heads turned in their direction. Odelia felt herself blush. Perhaps she had gone a tad overboard with the wedding, but she'd waited fifty years for it, after all. "Thankfully, my sister is the epitome of good taste," she admitted sheepishly. "I think she kept me somewhat in line."

Phillip leaned over and kissed her cheek.

"Oh, Phillip, I'm so happy for you," Odelia told him warmly.

He looped an arm about her lacy pink shoulders and gave her a squeeze. "Thank you. Who knew responsibility would be such an adventure?"

Speaking of adventures, three of them ran up just then to tug at him.

"Come on, Daddy Phil," said little Grace. She looked like a doll in her layers of pale purple organza, a huge, floppy bow tied about her pale red head. "Mom says it's time."

"All right. Okay," Phillip said indulgently, getting to his feet. "Time for what?"

"To throw the flowers," said Tucker.

"The bouquet," Nathan corrected, adjusting his new glasses on his nose.

"They're gonna do it at our pool," Tucker announced proudly, "and all the single girls has got to go line up, even the aunties."

"Well, that leaves me out," Odelia said happily.

"Not me!" Grace trilled, clapping her hands and hopping in place.

"We'd better get you a good spot, then," Phillip told her. Reaching down, he grasped her by the waist and threw her up to sit on his shoulder, then they went galloping off for the French door that opened onto the patio at the end of the dining space, Grace giggling with delight, her organza skirts flopping. Tucker ran behind them, but Nathan paused to send Odelia a long-suffering look that didn't fool her in the least. He couldn't hide his happiness as he went off after them.

Odelia hurried to catch the arm of her husband, who was happy to abandon a conversation about the crisis in health care to escort his wife outside to watch the festivities. She had to bite her lip as the boys prodded Hypatia and Magnolia into line on either side of Grace, who couldn't even stand still in her excitement. Poor Hypatia tried her best to offer a gracious smile, but Magnolia barely managed not to look disgruntled. Dallas stood directly behind Grace, her hands placed lightly upon the girl's shoulders. Perhaps a dozen others crowded in behind them next to the sparkling pool, which Garrett Willows had decorated with plants from his garden shop, The Willow Tree.

Phillip delivered to his bride the silk version of the champagne rose and ivy bouquet that Carissa had carried at the church, both creations of Jessa Willows. He kissed her then grasped her by the shoulders and physically turned her back to the group of single women waiting to catch the bouquet. Carissa closed her eyes, lowered the bouquet and flung the flowers backward over her head. They soared half the length of the pool and dropped straight toward little Grace, only to pass over her head. Dallas reflexively lifted her hands, palms up, only to have the bouquet bounce off them and fly over the heads of several others to land in the pool, where they floated prettily for several seconds while everyone gasped then finally laughed.

"Perhaps we're to have a respite from romance at Chatam House," Hypatia said hopefully, coming to stand beside Odelia, even as Carissa apologized to Dallas and Phillip used the pool net to drag in the bouquet.

Dallas shrugged and laughed, but Odelia's heart went out to the girl. Dallas was such a romantic. Perhaps she was a tad exuberant, a bit dramatic, but Odelia was the last one to hold that against the girl. Surely God had someone in mind for her niece. She just wasn't cut out to live alone. Then again, God knew best, as He constantly proved.

Just look at what He had wrought this time. Odelia watched as Tucker and Grace pitched in to rescue the silk bouquet, plucking it from the pool net and mopping it with a thick beach towel. Nathan had the good sense to rescue the thing before they beat it to pieces. He presented it to Dallas with a slight bow. She accepted the poor thing with a smile, holding it out to one side, as it still leaked. Phillip and Carissa watched arm in arm, as proud as any parents could be. Meanwhile, Murdock and Maryanne watched them, expressions of utter joy on their faces.

Nathan escorted Dallas toward the house. As they passed by, Murdock laid a hand on the boy's shoulder and fell in beside him. Between them, Phillip and Murdock would provide everything any boy could ever need in the way of male guidance.

Sighing happily, Odelia patted her husband Kent's belly then reached up to straighten his pink bow tie. Yes, indeed, God's plans were always best, and if He chose to make Chatam House a center of romance, who was she to object? After all, spreading love and joy to the world through the doors of Chatam House was not such a bad thing. Perhaps it was not a grand ministry like that of their older brother Hub, a retired pastor now, or a clear calling like that of their nephew Morgan, a professor at Buffalo Creek Bible College. But three old ladies could do worse. Much worse. And it wouldn't be nearly so much fun.

Odelia giggled as Kent sneaked a kiss at the same time as the bride and groom did.

Not nearly so much fun or so sweet.

* * * * *

Dear Reader,

Change is a constant fact of life. Some change is sudden and wrenching. Some change, like growing older, comes upon us so gradually that we don't even realize it's happening.

I'm always intrigued by the ways God chooses to make changes in our lives. He can blind us with His glory, as He did Paul on the road to Damascus, or He can work subtly in our hearts, one moment, one need, one challenge, one desire at a time.

Like Phillip Chatam, we all feel, at some point, that we are beneath God's notice, but it's never true. He's always ready, always shaping circumstances, to change what needs to be changed to bring us into His will, where true happiness is to be found.

All we have to do is ask. Have you asked to be conformed to God's will? Do it, and live your own story.

I hope you've enjoyed reading the Chatam House series as much as I've enjoyed writing it. Be sure to look for the next Chatam book, featuring Morgan Chatam, later in 2014.

God bless,

Arlene James

## Questions for Discussion

1. Grief support groups are designed to help those whose loved ones have died. Do you think that men or women are more inclined to join grief support groups? Why? Both Phillip and Carissa were reluctant to participate in the group. Why do you think that was? Have you ever joined a support group of any kind? Was it a positive or negative experience?

2. Phillip once remarked to his parents that he didn't think of his life in terms of a career but rather in terms of experiences. What is the difference? If you were advising a young person preparing for the future, would you tell him or her to think in terms of career or experiences?

3. Not only did Phillip believe that God was too busy to pay attention to someone as unremarkable and self-centered as him but that He really didn't want to hear from him. Have you ever felt this way?

4. Carissa believed that being a single mom prevented her from finding a man who was will-

ing to love her and her three children. Do you agree with this? Why or why not?

5. Nathan seemed to resent any man who was interested in his mother romantically. Why do you think this was? How did Phillip handle this? What would you have done in his place?

6. Without a college degree in a difficult economy, Carissa found it hard to find a regular job with a good salary. Did her work-at-home job seem like the best idea? What made it difficult for Carissa? Why?

7. Phillip feared that he had nothing to offer Carissa and her children and was reticent to get too close to them. Why do you think he felt this way?

8. Carissa's mother, Alexandra, tried to help her daughter by offering to take custody of Grace. Why was Carissa upset by this? Why do you think Alexandra thought this was a good idea? What would you have done in this situation?

9. When Phillip's parents, Murdock and Maryanne, came to town, Phillip was nervous that they wouldn't like Carissa or her children.

Why was he so concerned about his parents' approval? Do you seek out your parents' approval when you date someone? Explain.

10. Carissa and Phillip made good partners in their smartphone app business. Do you think mixing one's business and personal life is a good idea? Have you ever done so? How did it work out?